"Come back to the ranch with me. I'll help you. You'll be safe."

He reached over and took her hand, squeezing it gently, and she was reminded of last night when he had pulled her through the rodeo crowd. "You shouldn't have to do this alone. I promise. I won't let anything happen to you."

Tanner pulled her to a stop and turned her to face him. "There is something I have to tell you. Last night when I saw you...I felt this strong connection as if you were some missing part of me and when I saw you it was like this jolt...." He stopped and looked embarrassed.

She cupped his strong jaw with her free hand and smiled as she looked into his eyes. "I don't think you're crazy. I felt it, too."

"Then come back with me—"

"I can't. I have to go. I have no choice." Her heart ached at the thought of never seeing him again. But if she wanted to protect him, she *had* to leave. Whatever had happened between them, she couldn't put Tanner and his family in jeopardy any more than she already had.

USA TODAY Bestselling Author

B.J. DANIELS

LASSOED

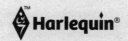
Harlequin®

TORONTO NEW YORK LONDON
AMSTERDAM PARIS SYDNEY HAMBURG
STOCKHOLM ATHENS TOKYO MILAN MADRID
PRAGUE WARSAW BUDAPEST AUCKLAND

The one thing no one told me was how many good writer friends I would make on this journey. This one is for Amanda Stevens, who is always there when I need her. I should add, she is also the scariest person I know and if you don't believe it, wait until you read her new Graveyard series.

ISBN-13: 978-0-373-74603-3

LASSOED

Recycling programs for this product may not exist in your area.

Copyright © 2011 by Barbara Heinlein

ABOUT THE AUTHOR

USA TODAY bestselling author B.J. Daniels wrote her first book after a career as an award-winning newspaper journalist and author of thirty-seven published short stories. That first book, *Odd Man Out,* received a four-and-a-half-star review from *RT Book Reviews* and went on to be nominated for Best Intrigue for that year. Since then she has won numerous awards, including a career achievement award for romantic suspense and many nominations and awards for best book.

Daniels lives in Montana with her husband, Parker, and two springer spaniels, Spot and Jem. To contact her, write to B.J. Daniels, P.O. Box 1173, Malta, MT 59538 or email her at bjdaniels@mtintouch.net. Check out her website at www.bjdaniels.com.

Books by B.J. Daniels

*Whitehorse, Montana
†Whitehorse, Montana:The Corbetts
**Whitehorse, Montana:Winchester Ranch
††Whitehorse, Montana:Winchester Ranch Reloaded
‡Whitehorse, Montana:Chisholm Cattle Company

CAST OF CHARACTERS

Tanner Chisholm—The cowboy knows the moment he sees the woman at the rodeo that she is in serious trouble—and that fate has sent her to him.

Billie Rae Rasmussen—She is running for her life when she runs right into the cowboy's arms.

Duane Rasmussen—The husband has everything on his side—including the law.

Marshall Chisholm—The rancher is just in the wrong place at the wrong time and it will cost him.

Emma Chisholm—The fourth wife of Hoyt Chisholm is determined to prove her husband's innocence—even if the cost is her life.

Hoyt Chisholm—Was it just bad luck? Or is he hiding the truth about his deceased wives?

Aggie Wells—How far will the former insurance investigator go to prove Hoyt Chisholm is a killer?

Krystal Blake Chisholm—She disappeared almost thirty years ago. What are the chances she will turn up now?

Sheriff McCall Crawford—The newlywed has her hands full even before another person goes missing.

Chapter One

The lights came out of the darkness like an oasis in the desert. Billie Rae glanced at the gas gauge on the old pickup, then in her rearview mirror.

She hadn't seen a vehicle behind her for miles now, but she didn't slow down, didn't dare. The pickup engine roared loudly, the speedometer clocked at over a hundred, but it was the gas gauge that had her worried.

She was almost out of fuel. Which meant she was also out of luck.

At the speed she was traveling, the lights ahead were coming up fast. At first she thought it was a small town. She hadn't seen one for more than fifty miles. But as she sped toward the glittering lights, she realized it wasn't a town. It appeared to be a fairgrounds aglow with lights.

Suddenly fireworks shot up from the horizon, bursting in the huge ebony sky stretched over this vast Montana prairie. She stared in surprise, realizing with a start what day it was. July 2. Two days away from the Fourth. She let the pickup slow to eighty as the booming fireworks burst around her, momentarily blinding her. The engine coughed. She glanced at the gas gauge. The pickup was running on fumes.

In her headlights she caught sight of the sign to the Whitehorse fairgrounds and another sign that announced Rodeo July 2–4. As the pickup engine coughed again, Billie Rae knew she'd just run out of options as well as gas.

She turned onto the dirt road that had a handmade sign that read Rodeo Parking and let the pickup coast in past dozens of trucks and horse trailers parked in the field around the rodeo arena. Just as the engine died, she pulled the truck into a spot between two pickups and turned off the headlights.

The highway she'd just come down had been nothing but blackness in her rearview mirror. Now, though, she wasn't surprised to see a set of headlights in the far distance.

She'd known she didn't have much of a head start. Just as she'd known nothing short of dying would keep him from coming after her.

Billie Rae sat for a moment fighting tears. Her chest ached from the sudden loss of hope. Without gas she wasn't going any farther—as if she really believed she could ever go far enough to get away from Duane. She slumped over the steering wheel.

She'd left the house with only the clothes on her back, and now it was just a matter of minutes before he found her. Duane was no fool. He'd know the pickup would be running low on gas by now and that she hadn't stopped to fill it up since she had no money. She'd had to leave her purse behind—not that there was any money in it, thanks to Duane. He had kept her a virtual prisoner since their wedding six months ago.

None of that mattered now, though. She should never have run. Duane was right. There was no getting away from him. He'd get a good laugh out of her thinking she could. Hadn't he said he would follow her to the ends of the earth?

But it was what else he'd said when she'd

told him she wanted out of the marriage that made her now begin to tremble in the dark cab of the pickup.

He had grabbed her by the throat and thrown her down on the bed. "You ever leave me and I will hunt you down like a mad dog and hurt you in ways you can't even imagine."

Her heart began to pound now with both fear and outrage. Duane had been so sweet, so loving, so caring before the wedding. Her mother had just died and she'd needed someone strong to lean on. Duane had provided the broad shoulder. He'd helped her through a tough time.

And then she'd made the mistake of marrying him. It wasn't that he'd suddenly changed. It was that once he put that ring on her finger, he'd finally revealed who he really was—a bully, a bastard, a batterer.

Her hands were shaking as she let go of the steering wheel. Her fingers ached from gripping it so tightly. Was she just going to sit here and wait for him to find her? He'd done his best to beat her down, but there was still a little fight left in her. She'd left him, hadn't she? That proved she had more courage than she'd thought and certainly more than Duane had thought.

She wasn't going back. Nor was she going to let Duane kill her. She had been a young, foolish, enamored woman when she'd married him, but once she'd seen behind the mask to the monster, there was no going back after that. She wasn't one of those women who thought their husbands would change. Or that it was her fault when her husband took out his bad moods on her.

But there was no denying she was in trouble.

Opening the door, Billie Rae climbed out of the pickup, surprised how weak her knees felt. Between booms of fireworks she heard a vehicle slowing on the highway before the small community fairgrounds. She didn't dare look and what was the point? She knew who it was.

She quickly worked her way through the pickups and horse trailers, following the sound of the oohs and ahs of the audience in the stands as the fireworks continued to explode over her head. The fireworks were going off closer together. One huge boom rattled in her chest after another. Soon the crowd would be dispersing and leaving.

She felt all her bravado leave as well. Soon everyone would be gone. Maybe she could find a place to hide where Duane wouldn't... Who was she kidding? Duane was going to find her, and when he did...

Glancing back through the parked vehicles, she caught a glimpse of a large black car driving slowly into the lot. Duane. He'd find the old classic Chevy pickup that had been his father's pride and joy. He'd find her.

She raced behind the grandstand in blind panic, knowing what he would do when he found her. She shouldn't have tried to leave him. She should have waited until she had a plan. But when Duane had come home earlier and she'd seen the rage building in him, she'd known how the evening would end and she couldn't let him hurt her again.

Billie Rae ran, blinded by tears and terror. If she could reach the stands, maybe she could disappear into the crowd—at least temporarily. Eventually, though, the stands would clear out and all that would be left would be her—and Duane.

As she came around the end of the grandstand, she collided with a tall cowboy. She'd been running for her life, glancing back over her shoulder and not looking where she was going, so she was hit hard, with her breath knocked out of her and her feet out from under her. If he hadn't caught her, she would have fallen to the ground.

"Easy," the cowboy said, his big hands gripping her shoulders to steady her. Tears continued to spill and she couldn't quit trembling. She opened her mouth to speak but nothing came out as she looked up into the man's handsome face.

He was dressed in boots, jeans and a fancy Western shirt. A gray Stetson was tilted back on his dark head. But it was the kindness in his brown eyes that had her riveted as the fireworks' grand finale continued.

Huge booms reverberated through her as brilliant colors showered the sky around the two of them in breathtaking beauty. For a few moments, it seemed they were the only two people in the world. As if this show was only for them alone. The cowboy smiled down at her and she felt a hitch in her chest.

The fireworks show ended in hushed dark silence, then the large lights of the fairgrounds blinked on and Billie Rae heard the crunch of gravel under a boot heel at the other end of the large grandstand.

As if coming out of a dream, she swung her gaze to where a dark figure was heading their way. Duane. She would recognize that arrogant gait anywhere.

She tried to pull away from the cowboy, needing to run, but he held on tight to her as the crowd suddenly swarmed around them.

TANNER CHISHOLM WOULD HAVE scoffed at even the idea of love at first sight—until a few moments ago. When the woman had come running out of the darkness behind the grandstand and into his arms in a shower of fireworks, noise and beautiful lights, he'd taken one look at her face and fallen.

Time froze with fireworks going off all around them. When she'd crashed into him he felt as if his whole life had been leading up to that moment. He'd known in an instant that it was no accident that this woman had run into his arms on this warm summer night.

He stared into her wide brown eyes, as her dark curly hair floated around her shoulders. He saw the terror etched in her tear-streaked face, felt her trembling and realized that come hell or high water, he'd do his damnedest to move heaven and earth for this woman.

It was crazy, wonderful and totally out of character. He wasn't the kind of man who fell in love in a split second. But any man would have seen that this woman was running for her life.

"What's wrong?" he asked as she fought to pull away from him and run. He saw her look behind him again. A man was headed in their direction, fighting the crowd to get to them in a way that left no doubt the man was furious—and coming after the woman in Tanner's arms.

"Come with me." Tanner took her hand and pulled her through the crowd. He knew these rodeo grounds like the back of his hand because he'd grown up here, played under these grandstands, ridden in junior rodeo and had later ridden bucking broncs out in the arena.

The woman resisted for only a moment before she let him lead her through the crowd and the darkness toward the shadowy fairground buildings beyond the rodeo arena. From the way she was still trembling, he suspected that the man chasing her meant to hurt her. Or at least she thought so. The fact that she was more afraid of the man than a complete stranger told him the woman was desperate.

As he drew her between two of the fair buildings, he spotted the man fighting his way through the rodeo crowd. Tanner caught the man's expression under one of the large lights. The heightened fury he saw on the man's face made him worry he might have made things worse for the woman by trying to protect her.

Too late now. Whatever had the man all riled up, he wasn't going to be taking it out on this woman. Not tonight, anyway.

Tanner led her between two more buildings, weaving his way through the maze of dark structures, until he reached one he knew would be unlocked. Pulling the door open, he drew her inside, closed the door and turned the lock.

"Who is that out there?" he whispered, still holding her hand in the blackness inside the building.

Silence, then a hoarsely whispered, "My husband."

Tanner mentally gave himself a swift kick. He really had stepped in it this time. Only a fool jumped into a domestic argument. "Why's he so angry?"

She started to answer but he felt her freeze as she heard the same sound he did. Someone was running in this direction on the wooden boardwalk in front of the buildings. He didn't have to tell her to be quiet. He knew she was holding her breath.

The footfalls came to a stop outside the building, the last along the row. Past it was a line of huge cottonwoods cloaked in darkness. With luck, the man would think that was where they had gone.

Tanner could hear the man's heavy breathing and cursing, then his angry voice as he muttered, "You may have gotten away this time, Billie Rae, but this isn't over. When I find you, I'm going to make you wish you were dead. That's if I don't kill you with my bare hands."

The man stood outside the door panting hard, then his footfalls ebbed away back the way he'd come. The woman he'd called Billie Rae let go of Tanner's hand, and he could hear her fumbling with the door lock.

"Not so fast," Tanner said, reaching around her to turn on the light. They were both blinded for a moment by the sudden light. "I think you'd better tell me what's going on, because you heard what he just said. That man plans to hurt you. If he hasn't already," Tanner added as he saw the fading bruise around her left eye.

WHAT BILLIE RAE HAD HEARD her husband say wasn't anything new. He'd threatened her plenty of times before, and the threats, she'd learned the hard way, weren't empty ones.

"I appreciate what you did for me, but I can't involve you in this," she said, finally finding her voice.

The cowboy let out a humorless laugh. "I'm already involved up to my hat. Do you have someplace you can go? Family? Friends?"

Billie Rae opened her mouth to lie. Duane had moved her away from what little family and friends she'd had right after the wedding. She'd lost contact over the past six months.

Duane had made sure of that. Just as he had thrown a fit when she'd suggested going back to work.

"Your work is in this house, taking care of me. That's your work."

"You don't have anyone you can call, do you?" the cowboy said. "Don't worry. It's going to be all right. I know a place you can stay where you will be safe."

Billie Rae wanted desperately to take the cowboy up on his offer but realized she couldn't. It had been bad enough when Duane had been after her alone. Now he would be looking for the cowboy he'd seen her with. "No, you don't understand. Duane will come after *you* now. I'm so sorry. I should never have put you in this position."

"You didn't. I'm the one who dragged you in here," he said as he pulled out his cell phone.

She tried to protest to whatever he was about to do, but he shushed her.

"I need a ride," he said into the phone.

She heard laughter on the other end.

"I need you to bring me my pickup. That's right, it's parked right where we left it before the rodeo. No, I can't come get it myself, Marshall, or I wouldn't have called you. The keys are in it. I'm in the last fairground building. There will be two of us. Make it quick, okay?" He snapped off the phone and gave her a reassuring smile.

Billie Rae wondered if she'd just jumped from the skillet into the fire. But there was something about this man that made her feel safe. It wasn't just the kindness she saw in his brown eyes.

There was a softness to his voice and his movements that belied his size and the strength she could see in his broad shoulders, muscled arms and callused hands.

This was a man who did manual labor— not one who either sat behind a desk or rode around all day in a car.

"I'm Tanner Chisholm," he said and held out his hand.

"Billie Rae Johnson." She realized she'd given him her maiden name instead of her married one.

"My brother Marshall is coming to pick us up in my truck, then we'll go out to the ranch where my stepmother, Emma, will make you feel at home. She'll insist you have something to eat. She does that to everyone. Humor her; it is much easier in the long run." He smiled. "You'll like Emma. Everyone does."

"I couldn't possibly impose—"

"Trust me, it is impossible to impose at the Chisholm ranch. If anything, Emma and my father, Hoyt, will want to adopt you."

She felt tears well and quickly brushed them away. "Why are you being so nice to me? You don't know me."

"I know you're in trouble and I'm a sucker for a woman who needs my help," he joked. "Seriously, whatever is going on, you need someplace to stay tonight at least and to give your husband a chance to calm down."

As if Duane was going to calm down, she thought with a grimace. All of this would have him foaming at the mouth with fury.

"I assume you drove to the rodeo?"

"A pickup. It's out of gas. But—"

"My brother and I will see to it tomorrow. It will be safe here tonight."

Maybe the truck would be safe but the brothers wouldn't be if they came to fetch it tomorrow. Duane would be watching it and waiting.

She had to stop this now. She knew Duane, knew what he would do to this cowboy. "You have to let me go," she said as she reached for the doorknob again. "You don't know my husband. He'll come after you—"

"I think I *do* know your husband," Tanner said and gently touched her cheek under her left eye with his fingertips. She flinched, not because her bruised cheek still hurt, but because she'd forgotten about her healing black eye and now this kind cowboy knew her hidden shame.

At the sound of a truck pulling up outside the building, Tanner said, "That will be Marshall." He opened the door a crack and looked out as if checking to make sure the coast was clear. "I come from a large ranch family that sticks together. I have five brothers. Your husband isn't going to take on the six of us, trust me."

Before she could argue, he quickly ushered her out to a large ranch truck. She noticed the sign printed on the side: Chisholm Cattle Company. Tanner opened the truck door, then taking her waist in both of his large hands, lifted her in before sliding into the bench seat next to her.

"Marshall, meet Billie Rae. Billie Rae, my big brother Marshall."

The cowboy behind the wheel grinned. Like his brother, Marshall had dark hair and brown eyes reflecting his Native American ancestry. Both men were very handsome but there was also something kind and comforting in their faces.

"I'd appreciate it if you got this truck moving," Tanner said, glancing in his side mirror. He turned back to Billie Rae, plucked a cowboy hat from the gun rack behind her and dropped it onto her long, dark, curly hair.

Marshall laughed. "So you got yourself into some kind of trouble and apparently involved this pretty little lady in the midst of it, huh?" He shook his head, but he got the truck moving.

As they drove out the back way of the fairgrounds, Billie Rae stared through the windshield from under the brim of the hat, afraid she'd see Duane in the dispersing crowd. Or worse, Duane would see her—and the name of the ranch painted on the side of the truck.

Chapter Two

Duane Rasmussen leaned against his father's pickup, arms crossed over his chest, his heart pounding with both anger and anticipation.

The fairgrounds were still clearing out. His head hurt from searching the crowd and waiting to see Billie Rae's contrite face.

She would come crawling back, apologizing and saying how sorry she was. She'd be a lot sorrier when he got through with her. The thought kicked up his pulse to a nice familiar throb he could feel in his thick neck.

As his daddy used to say, "A man who can't control his woman is no man at all."

He used to think his old man was a mean SOB. But Duane hadn't understood what his father had to contend with when it came to living with a woman. Sometimes just opening the door and seeing Billie Rae with that look on her face…

Duane couldn't describe it any other way than as a deer-in-the-headlights look. It made him want to wipe it off her face. He hated it when she acted as if she had to fear him.

He had told her repeatedly that he loved her and that the only reason he had to get tough with her sometimes was because she made him mad. Or when she acted like she was walking around on eggshells, treating him as if she thought he might go off at any moment and slap her.

Didn't he realize how that would make him even angrier with her?

Duane shook his head now. He'd never be able to understand his wife.

Like this little trick she'd just pulled, taking off on him. What the hell was she thinking? She'd been so sweet and compliant when they were dating. She'd liked it when he took care of her, told her what was best for her, didn't bother her with making any of the decisions.

He couldn't understand what had changed her. It was a mystery to him especially since he'd given the woman everything—she didn't even have to work outside the home.

He'd squashed all talk of her looking for a job after they'd moved. No wife of his was working. Every man knew that working outside the home ruined a woman. They got all kinds of strange ideas into their heads. Let a woman be too independent and you were just asking for trouble.

With a curse, he saw that the parking area was almost empty. Only a few stragglers wandered out from the direction of the rodeo grandstands. The rodeo cowboys had loaded up their stock and taken off. The parking lot in the field next to the fairgrounds was empty.

A sliver of worry burrowed under his skin. Where was Billie Rae? Still hiding in those trees to the west of the fairgrounds? The night air was cooling quickly. She wasn't dressed for spending the night in the woods, not this far north in Montana.

That was another thing that puzzled him, the way she'd taken off. She hadn't planned this as far as he could tell. He'd found her purse and her house key. She hadn't even taken a decent jacket, and it appeared she'd left with nothing more than the clothes on her back. How stupid was that?

He settled in to wait. When she got cold and hungry she'd come back to the pickup. She'd know he would be waiting for her, so she'd come with her tail between her legs. He smiled at the thought. Of course Billie Rae would come back. Where else could she go?

EMMA CHISHOLM TOOK ONE LOOK at the woman her stepson had brought home from the rodeo and recognized herself—thirty years ago. It gave her a start to have a reminder show up at her front door after all these years.

All of it was too familiar, the terror in the young woman's eyes, the fading bruises, the insecurity and indecision in her movements and the panic and pain etched in her face.

The worst part, Emma knew, was the memory of the tearful promises that would be forgotten in an instant the next time. But it was those tender moments that gave every battered woman hope that this time, her lover really would never do it again. They called it the honeymoon period. It came right before the next beating—and that beating was always worse than the one before.

It made her heart ache just to look at the woman. A part of Emma wanted to distance herself, deny that she had been this young woman, but if there was one thing she'd learned, it was that all things circled back at you for a reason.

"This is Billie Rae Johnson," Tanner said. "Her car broke down at the rodeo. I told her we had plenty of room and that we'd get her fixed up in the morning."

Emma smiled and held out her hand to the young woman. "I'm Emma. We are delighted to have you stay with us as long as you'd like." Her gaze shifted to Tanner.

He'd never been one to exaggerate or lie, but she didn't believe his story for a moment. Billie Rae was on the run. Emma knew the look, remembered it only too well. Her heart went out to Billie Rae.

"I don't want to be an imposition." Billie Rae was a beauty, but Emma knew that her stepson had seen beyond that. Tanner was like his father, who brought home those in need. Was that one reason Hoyt had fallen in love with her? Because he'd seen the need in Emma herself?

"I promise you it is no imposition," Emma said. "I love having guests, especially female ones. I'm so outnumbered around here."

"Thank you," Billie Rae said. She looked exhausted. No doubt she'd been running on adrenaline and fear for hours and was about to crash.

"Why don't I show you up to one of our many guest rooms?" Emma said quickly. "Since all six of the boys have their own places now, we have more empty bedrooms than you can shake a stick at. Then I'll get you a snack. It always helps me sleep."

Billie Rae glanced at Tanner, who smiled and nodded, then she followed Emma without a word.

"You have this whole wing to yourself," Emma said when they reached one of the rooms that was always made up for guests. "So please, make yourself at home and if there is anything you need, don't hesitate to ask."

"I won't be here more than tonight."

Emma smiled. "Get some rest. Sometimes

it takes more than a night. You are welcome to stay as long as you need. You're safe here."

Billie Rae nodded, tears coming to her eyes. "You're very kind."

"No, I've been where you are right now." Admitting it was easier than she'd thought it would be.

For a moment, the young woman looked as if she was going to deny it or pretend she didn't know what Emma was talking about.

"I was with a man who kicked the hell out of me on a regular basis," Emma said, surprised how easily too the anger came back. "Oh sure, he was always sorry. It was for my own good. He loved me. It took me a while to realize it wasn't for my own good, just as it wasn't my fault and that nothing I did or could do would change him. He didn't love me. He didn't know what love was."

Tears spilled over Billie Rae's cheeks. "I'm just so embarrassed."

Emma took her hand and they sat down on the edge of the bed. "Embarrassed? Oh, sweetie, you have done nothing to be embarrassed about."

"I married the wrong man. He...fooled me."

She nodded. "But you got smart and left him."

"He told me he'll kill me and I don't doubt it," Billie Rae said, brushing angrily at her tears.

Emma shook her head. "He isn't going to find you here. Tomorrow you can decide what to do next."

"You don't know Duane. I'm afraid he'll find out that you all helped me and do something terrible to you."

"Honey, that's why there's a shotgun in this house. Trust Tanner. He's a good man." She studied the young woman for a moment. "I don't know if you believe in fate or not, but I can tell you this. Tanner finding you and bringing you here was no accident."

AS DUANE SAT IN THE empty fairgrounds in the dark, he knew where he'd made his mistake. If he'd gotten Billie Rae pregnant right away, none of this would be happening. But instead he'd listened to his wife, who'd wanted to wait until they were "settled in as a couple," as she called it.

With a surge of angry resentment, he realized

she just wanted to make sure the marriage was to her liking. That *he* was to her liking.

Duane swore under his breath. Wait until he got his hands on her. He'd show her. She would never pull a stunt like this again. He'd kill her if she did. That was if he didn't end up killing her this time. He flushed, embarrassed to be put in this position, as the scent of fried food still drifted on the breeze coming through the open window of his Lincoln.

The last of the lights of the rodeo vehicles had dimmed away to darkness in the distance, all headed west. From the faint glow on the horizon, Duane figured the closest Montana town had to be up the highway. He was hungry and tired and even his anger couldn't keep him going much longer.

Duane looked around. It was just his car now and his father's pickup.

Where the hell was Billie Rae?

He waited until the night air cooled to a chill before he put up his car window, started the engine and drove down to park by the pickup. Billie Rae would be coming back soon and he didn't want to miss her.

A thought struck him like a blow. Unless she'd left with someone.

That cowboy he'd seen her with?

He couldn't get his mind around that. But then he'd thought he'd made it clear to Billie Rae what would happen to her if she ever tried to leave him—or to anyone who helped her. She'd made a friend who thought she could come between them. That friend was no longer anywhere around, now, was she?

Duane had thought Billie Rae had learned her lesson that time. But apparently that hadn't stopped her from "befriending" someone else who thought they could interfere in his marriage to her.

None of this was like Billie Rae, he thought as the hours wore on, and he felt an uncertainty that rattled him. For the first time, he wasn't sure he knew his wife as well as he thought he did.

AFTER HER TALK WITH Emma Chisholm, Billie Rae showered, slipped into the cotton nightgown left for her on the huge bed and slid between the sheets that smelled like fresh air.

Emma had also left her a glass of milk and a plate of sliced homemade banana bread. Billie Rae had eaten all of it. She hadn't realized how hungry she was or that she hadn't eaten since breakfast that morning.

For the first time in a long time, she felt as if she could breathe as she got up to brush her teeth with the new toothbrush Emma had set out for her. The cool night air blew in through the open window next to her bed as she crawled back under the covers. The breeze billowed the sheer white curtains. She could see the outline of mountains in the distance, smell sage and hay beyond the fresh clean scent of the line-dried linens on the bed.

But it was the sweet scent of freedom that she gulped in as if she was a drowning woman finally coming up for air. She was still half-afraid to believe it, but lying here in this house, she was filled with a sense of peace like none she had felt since she'd married Duane.

Don't rest too easy. I'm still out here looking for you. And when I find you—

She took another deep breath, chasing away the sound of Duane's voice. Like Scarlett

O'Hara, she wouldn't think about tomorrow. For tonight, she was alive and safe, and that was more than she had hoped for.

At a tap at her door, she said, "Come in," thinking it would be Emma.

"I just wanted to check on you and make sure you have everything you need," Tanner said, peeking around the door.

"I'm fine." More than fine. "Thank you."

"I'll see you in the morning, then," he said. "I'll be just down the hall."

She couldn't help her surprise. Emma said that all the Chisholm sons had their own places now. "I thought—"

"I decided to stay here tonight." He shrugged, looking a little embarrassed. "In case you..."

"Needed anything," she finished for him, smiling.

"Good night, then," he said and closed the door.

Billie Rae lay in the bed still smiling, remembering what Emma had said. Trust Tanner. She did. She closed her eyes, dead tired, aching for sleep, but quickly opened them as Duane's image appeared as if waiting to taunt her in a nightmare.

Trust Tanner? Do you really think that cowboy or his whole damned family can save you?

She touched her diamond engagement ring in the darkness, the thick band of white gold next to it a reminder of who she was. Mrs. Duane Rasmussen, as if she could forget it.

Were you listening to that preacher? Till death do us part, Billie Rae. And that, sweet-heart, is the way it is going to be, come hell or high water. You understand me, or am I going to have to refresh your memory?

As she spun the band in a circle, she thought about what Emma had said about fate. Did she believe in fate? Tanner had saved her tonight, he'd brought her to this house, to his step-mother, Emma, who had known instinctively what Billie Rae was going through.

Maybe fate had brought her together with this family tonight, but Billie Rae knew she had to run again come morning.

Slowly she took off the rings to set them on the bedside table. The diamond winked at her in the light of the star-filled night coming in through the sheer, billowing curtains.

You really think it's that easy to be rid of me?

She got up, stood in the middle of the room, unsure what to do with the rings. Her first impulse was to throw them away, but common sense won out. The rings were worth money and she was going to need some if she hoped to stay free of Duane. She put them in the pocket of her slacks.

As she climbed back into the bed and pulled the covers up, she felt stronger than she had since she married Duane. It had been fate that she'd met Tanner Chisholm and that he'd brought her to this house. She'd been ready to give up and go back to Duane, believing she had no choice.

But now she felt as if she could do this. She *would* do this. She had let Duane Rasmussen bully her for too long.

This time when she closed her eyes she pictured Tanner Chisholm's face. But she didn't kid herself that Duane wouldn't be nearby waiting to ruin her sleep.

TANNER WOKE TO SCREAMING. He bolted upright in bed, confused for a moment where he was. As everything came back in a rush, he swung his legs over the side of the bed, pulled on his jeans and ran barefoot down the hall.

His conscious mind told him it was impossible that Billie Rae's husband had found her here. That there was no way the man could be in the house. Worse, that he could have found the bedroom where she slept and—

He shoved open the door. Faint light shone through the sheer curtains at the large window next to her bed. A shaft of light from the hallway shot across the floor, making a path into the room. Tanner felt his heart break at the sounds coming from the bed. He rushed to Billie Rae.

She came out of the dream swinging her arms wildly. He didn't have to guess who she was trying to fight off.

"It's me, Billie Rae. Tanner. Tanner Chisholm."

Her eyes were wild with panic. She blinked at the sound of his voice and slowly focused on his face in the dim light before bursting into tears.

"You had a bad dream, but you're all right," he said as he sat down on the bed and pulled her into his arms. As he stroked her hair, he whispered, "It's all right. You're safe. You're all right."

She clung to him, sobbing, her breathing ragged. He could feel her damp cotton nightgown against his bare chest. She was shivering uncontrollably from the cold, from whatever horror still clung to her from the nightmare.

He held her close, continuing to stroke her hair and whisper words of comfort while all the time he wanted to kill the man who'd hurt this woman.

"Your nightgown is damp with sweat," he said after her breathing became more normal. Shadows played on the walls, the breeze whipped the sheer curtains and outside the window, a branch scraped against the house.

As he started to pull away, she cried, "Please, don't leave me."

"I'll be right back. I'm just going to get you something warm and dry to sleep in." He hurried to his room, rummaged through a drawer where he'd left some of his old clothing. He found a large soft-worn T-shirt and hurried back to Billie Rae's room.

She was sitting up in the bed, clutching the

covers to her chest. He sat down on the edge of the bed next to her again. "Here, take off the nightgown and put this on." He turned his back. He heard her behind him struggling to get out of the damp nightgown and knew she was still trembling from her nightmare.

What had her husband done to her to make her so frightened? He recalled what he'd heard the man say outside the door at the fair-grounds. But he'd thought them merely angry words. It wasn't until he'd seen the bruised area around Billie Rae's eye that he'd realized why she was so afraid of her husband.

Now he heard her pull on the T-shirt and lay back against the headboard.

He turned to look at her, jolted again by that strong emotion he'd felt under the lights of the exploding fireworks. Her face was lovely in the faint starlight. He couldn't imagine her ever looking more beautiful or desirable. Or vulnerable.

"Do you think you'll be able to sleep now?" he asked, starting to get to his feet, knowing what could happen if he stayed.

Her hand shot out and grabbed his wrist. He slowly sat back down.

There was a pleading in her brown eyes, along with flecks of gold.

"You want me to stay?"

She swallowed and he could see the battle going on inside her reflected in those big eyes. As he looked down, he saw that she'd taken off her wedding rings. There was a wide white mark where they had been.

He raised his gaze to her eyes again. "Slide over. I'll hold you until you fall asleep."

He saw relief, gratitude and something he didn't dare think about too long in those eyes.

She slid over and he lay down next to her. She moved closer as if desperately needing to know he was still there. He put his arms around her and drew her to him. She fit against him perfectly. He nestled his head against the pillow of her dark, luxurious hair and breathed in her scent. She smelled of soap and summer. He closed his eyes, feeling the steady beat of his heart in sync with hers.

"Thank you," she whispered. "I'm sorry that I—"

"Shh," he whispered. "I'll be here as long as you need me."

BILLIE RAE WOKE IN THE wee hours of the morning from a wonderful dream. She lay very still, keeping her eyes closed as she tried to get back into the dream. But it stayed just out of reach, slipping further away, and she finally opened her eyes.

She thought she was at home, so when the horrible dread she always woke with settled over her, she closed her eyes again, pleading silently for the dream and the man in it who had made her feel so loved. Like in the dream, the arms around her didn't hold her as tightly as Duane's did. Tanner held her gently, not as if he feared she would get away, but more like he wanted to keep her safe.

With a start, she came fully awake. She *had* gotten away from Duane.

Tanner shifted in his sleep and for a moment she feared he would let her go. She had never met anyone like him. She hadn't dated all that much before she met Duane. In college, she'd had to get good grades to keep her scholarships and still help her mother, who had by then been diagnosed with cancer, so she'd had no time for a social life.

She'd never been held this tenderly, never

felt this safe and secure, never felt…the emotions she was experiencing at this moment—not even the first time she'd gone to bed with Duane. He'd been disappointed she wasn't a virgin and that had spoiled their lovemaking for both of them. After that, he was always much rougher as if he was punishing her for losing her virginity to the boy she'd dated all through high school and thought she was in love with.

Scott had been a nice boy, but just that—a boy. After high school, they'd gone to different colleges. They'd stayed in touch for a while, but had grown apart. Billie Rae had been thankful for that since she'd known by then that Scott wasn't the person she wanted to spend the rest of her life with.

She'd met Duane right after her mother died. Looking back, she saw that he had taken advantage of the vulnerable state she'd been in. She'd needed someone to lean on and Duane had made sure he was there, taking over her life, running it.

The problem was that when she no longer needed him in that way or wanted him to run her life, it was too late. By then, she'd needed

and wanted something different from him.
But Duane wasn't a giving, loving man. Nor
was he going to let her go. He'd whisked her
off to Vegas for a quickie marriage, selling it
as romantic.

Hadn't she known that night, standing in a
gaudy wedding chapel on the strip in front of
a justice of the peace and his wife, that she
was making a mistake? She remembered feeling as if she might faint. Duane had told her
she just needed food and that he would feed
her right after the ceremony.

Instead, they'd flown straight home as the
sun came up and he'd sprung the news on her.
They were moving to North Dakota.

Tanner shifted again in his sleep. Billie Rae
held her breath, afraid he would awaken and
leave her. A part of the dream returned, star-
tling her because there was no doubt that the
man in it had been Tanner Chisholm.

She sensed him coming awake and turned
in his arms to face him. It was still dark out.
In the faint starlight, she could see his bare
chest, a light sprinkling of dark hair that
formed a V disappear into the waistband of
his jeans.

She met his gaze and felt a bubble form in her chest. Her heart began to beat faster.

He started to pull away, but she cupped his jaw and he froze. "Billie Rae—"

Her thumb moved to his lips and she shook her head, her gaze holding his. She hadn't felt desire in a long time. It felt raw and powerful and urgent. Under normal circumstances she would have never acted upon it with a man she hardly knew.

She brushed a lock of dark hair back from Tanner's wonderful face, feeling as if she knew him soul-deep. Her fingers tingled at the touch. By the time the sun set tomorrow there was a good chance Duane would have caught up with her and, if not killed her, definitely hurt her.

There were some things she couldn't live with. Duane was one of them. The other was not acting on what she was feeling at this moment, knowing it might be her last day alive.

Slowly, she leaned toward Tanner and brushed a kiss over his lips. Her pulse thundered in her ears as he gently drew her to him. His kiss was light as the summer breeze coming through the window. His hands came up to cup her face in his warm, callused palms.

Desire burned through her veins like a runaway train on a downhill track. As the kiss deepened, his fingers burrowed into her wild mane of hair. She shoved back the covers, needing to feel the warmth of his body against her, desperate for his human touch after months of flinching whenever Duane reached for her.

Tanner drew her to him, rolling over on his back and pulling her on top of him. "Are you sure about this?" he whispered.

She kissed him, sat up and then grabbing the hem of the large T-shirt, she pulled it up over her head and tossed it away. She heard Tanner moan, and then his hands were cupping her breasts, his thumbs gently teasing her nipples, which were already hard as marbles.

He drew her down again, kissing her softly. She rolled off him and wriggled out of her panties, desperately needing to feel his warm flesh against hers. She heard him slip out of his jeans and then he was pulling her into his arms. He brushed a tendril of hair back from her cheek.

Their eyes locked as he slowly and sweetly began to make love to her.

Chapter Three

Duane woke in his car, cramped and out of sorts. He couldn't believe he'd had to spend the entire night in a fairgrounds parking lot in the middle of nowhere.

As he climbed out, he looked into the front seat of his father's classic pickup, expecting to see Billie Rae curled up there. He'd been so sure she would return, probably with some cowboy with a can of gas for the pickup and some romantic ideas for her.

But he hadn't heard a sound all night and the pickup front seat was empty. No Billie Rae. With a curse, Duane realized he was going to have to call his boss and ask for some time off.

As for his wife, he didn't know what to do. First, he supposed, he would search for her himself. Someone had to have seen her.

If that failed... Well, he might have to contact a couple of associates he'd met through his work. The nice thing about his job was that he met people who could and would do things for him that he'd rather not do himself. A little pressure here, a little pressure there, and people knew better than to say no to him.

He pulled out his cell phone, swearing under his breath as he punched in the number and asked for his boss. The last thing he'd do was admit the truth. He didn't want anyone to know what the bitch had done, how she'd made him look like a fool, let alone that he couldn't handle his own wife. He'd never live it down if his buddies found out about this. Other men lost respect for a man whose wife ran off on him.

No, he would take care of this himself and no one back home would be the wiser. That is, as long as he found Billie Rae fast. And one way or the other, he'd have to convince her never to pull something like this again. Either that or his lovely wife would end up dead, a terrible accident that would leave him a grieving widower—and free to find him a wife who knew her place.

He came up with a lame excuse, but his boss seemed to buy it. As he hung up, he told himself it was now time to deal with the mess Billie Rae had made. Walking around to the driver's side, Duane unlocked the pickup with his key and stared into it for a long moment, thinking about Billie Rae taking it. The truck had been his father's, purchased new almost fifty years before. His old man had loved this pickup and cared for it like a baby.

Hell, Duane had never even gotten to drive it until the old man died. His mother had been the one to give it to him—had his father known he was going to fall over dead with a heart attack he would have made other arrangements for his beloved classic pickup.

But Duane's mother hated the truck and resented the time and money and care the old man had put into it. She'd given it to Duane out of spite, knowing his father was now rolling over in his grave to think that his son had the truck. Which made Duane even angrier that Billie Rae had the impudence to take it.

The woman must be crazy. No one drove this pickup but him.

As he slid behind the wheel, he saw that she'd left the key in the ignition and swore. Her lack of respect… He couldn't wait to get his hands on her.

He reached to turn the key and saw that it was the spare he kept locked up. She'd broken into his desk? He hadn't even been aware she knew where he kept the spare key.

Duane felt that strange chill creep over him again. Billie Rae had been watching him, paying more attention than he'd thought.

He turned the key. The engine refused to turn over. That's when he saw the gas gauge. She'd run out of gas. That's why she'd stopped here.

The tap on his side window startled him. For an instant, he'd expected to see Billie Rae standing there instead of some old guy in a plaid shirt and a baseball cap.

"Trouble getting her started?" the old man asked.

Duane realized the man must be the caretaker in charge of the fairgrounds. He hadn't heard him drive up. Duane climbed out, pocketing the truck key. "The wife. She didn't check the gas gauge before she headed to the rodeo."

The old man laughed and shook his head. "I'm surprised you let her drive this. A 1962 Chevy Fleetside Shortbed with a Vortec 350, right?"

Duane nodded as he watched the caretaker run his hand over the hood. His old man had to be turning flips in his casket. He'd never let anyone touch his truck.

"You don't happen to have a few gallons of gas I could buy from you to get her into town, do you?" Duane asked.

"I haven't seen her around town," the man said frowning, still talking about the pickup. "You new to Whitehorse?"

So Whitehorse must be the closest town. "You could say that. If I had a hose, I could siphon some gas out of my car," Duane said impatiently.

"No need for that. I keep some extra gas for the lawnmower."

Duane followed the man back to a shed, waited while he unlocked the padlock on the door and went inside, returning with a small gas can that felt about half full.

"I'll bring this right back," he said, hoping the man wouldn't come with him. He hurried off, returning shortly, and handed the man the gas can and a twenty-dollar bill. "Thanks for your help." He had a thought. "Hey, is there any chance I could leave the pickup in one of your barns out here. My wife is tied up and I need to get back to her. I can't come back to get the truck for a while."

"No problem. You can just pull it in that one," the old man said pointing at the closest barn. "It will be plenty safe there until you can pick her up."

"Great," he started to turn away telling himself he had no choice since he couldn't drive two vehicles and who knew when he'd find Billie Rae. Nor did he want anyone else driving the truck.

"You're going to have to teach your wife to watch that gas gauge," the old man called after him with a chuckle.

He was going to have to teach his wife a lot of things when he found her.

"GOOD MORNING," BILLIE RAE said shyly from the kitchen doorway.

Tanner looked up. He'd been sitting at the kitchen table having a cup of coffee with Emma, who'd been chastising him.

He knew she was right. He'd fallen for a woman who was not just married—but in a very vulnerable state right now. He *should* have known better than to get more involved with her for not just his sake but hers as well.

When he met her gaze now, he was afraid he would see regret in her eyes. The morning light brought out the gold flecks in those eyes. With relief, he saw that they were free of regret. Their eyes locked and, after a moment, a slight flush came to her cheeks before she looked away.

They'd made love and fallen back to sleep in each other's arms. When he'd awakened this morning, she'd looked so beautiful and so serene lying there, he hadn't wanted to wake her.

He looked down into his coffee cup now, checking his expression as he felt Emma's watchful gaze on him. She'd already given him hell, telling him that she couldn't bear to see him get his heart broken and Billie Rae wasn't ready for another relationship.

"Sleep well?" Emma asked smiling as she handed Billie Rae a mug of coffee.

"Yes, thank you," Billie Rae said dropping her gaze and blushing as she took the mug and sat down in a chair across from Tanner.

Tanner smiled across the table at her. She looked a hundred percent better than she had last night at the rodeo. There was no longer that deer-in-the-headlights look in her eyes. Her long dark hair was still damp from her shower. He caught a whiff of her now too-familiar scent. She smelled heavenly. He couldn't help but think about their lovemaking and wish he had awakened her this morning.

Emma refilled his coffee cup, giving him another of her knowing looks. This one held a warning he couldn't ignore. He knew making love with Billie Rae shouldn't have happened. Legally, she was a married woman. But to his way of thinking, Duane had broken the vows, destroying that fragile thing that made a marriage.

He knew Emma was worried about him getting too close to Billie Rae and getting his heart broken. But he wondered if it wasn't already too late. Damned if he would ever regret what had happened between them, no matter what today brought. He didn't kid himself. He knew that Duane was still out there looking for Billie Rae—and that she knew it as well. Whatever was going to transpire between them, it wasn't over yet.

Emma kept up a cheerful chatter as she and the cook, Celeste, served homemade pancakes with huckleberry syrup. Tanner watched Billie Rae put away a dozen of the silver-dollar-sized cakes, smiling to himself. A good appetite was a sure sign that she was bouncing back.

"She doesn't want to hear any of this," Tanner said after Emma told a particularly funny story she'd heard about him as a boy. Billie Rae was smiling, looking relaxed, looking as if she belonged in this kitchen.

"I wish you'd gotten a chance to meet my husband Hoyt," Emma was saying. "He could tell you some stories about his boys.

But Hoyt's off digging fence post holes with Tanner's brothers."

Hoyt hadn't been home last night when Tanner and Marshall returned from the rodeo with Billie Rae. Tanner's father, according to Emma, had been at a ranchers' association meeting about some rustlers operating across the border in Wyoming.

It was odd, though, that Hoyt had already taken off so early this morning. Tanner hadn't even seen him before he left. His father had been putting in long hours recently, almost as if avoiding home.

He frowned at the thought and hoped everything was all right between his father and Emma. He and his brothers hadn't been happy when their father had sprung a new wife on them. But once they'd been around Emma for five minutes, they too had fallen in love with her.

Tanner was told she was nothing like Hoyt's other wives. He'd been too young to remember Laura, his father's first wife. She'd drowned in a boating accident. Tasha, his father's second wife, Tanner had heard was killed by a runaway horse.

A third wife, Krystal, had disappeared

shortly after Hoyt had brought her to the ranch. Tanner vaguely remembered her. After all that tragedy, his father had gone years without a woman in his life.

Then, out of the blue, he'd come home with Emma. She was older, closer to Hoyt's age, more full-figured, redheaded and had a fiery temper that had earned her respect from all of the men in the family. She'd changed things around here, but in a good way. And Tanner had never seen his father happier. Until recently, when he seemed to be avoiding being home.

"What would you like to do first this morning?" he asked Billie Rae after breakfast.

"Is there a pawnshop or jewelry store in White-horse?"

Tanner shook his head. "But there are several in Havre. I'd be happy to drive you."

"No, I couldn't possibly ask you—"

"You didn't ask. I'm volunteering, unless you need to go back to the fairgrounds for your vehicle?"

"The pickup I was driving isn't mine."

"Then I guess we don't need to worry about it."

She nodded but he saw the dark cloud move

over her eyes. She had a lot to worry about. They both did. She was worried about Duane, and Tanner was worried that this woman who had come crashing into his life would leave it just as suddenly.

"It's a nice drive to Havre," he said. "We'll have lunch and shop for whatever you need. I could use the day off, but don't tell my stepmother."

Emma swatted him as she passed.

Billie Rae nodded, tears in her eyes. "You have all been so kind. I really wish—"

"No regrets." Emma stopped next to her chair to lay a hand on her shoulder. "No tears, either, not on such a beautiful morning," she said. "You two best get goin'. Make sure Billie Rae gets whatever she needs in Havre." Emma pressed a wad of cash into Tanner's hand along with another silent warning look.

He was to make sure nothing happened to Billie Rae and that he didn't make things worse for her—as if he hadn't already.

"We'll be fine," he told his stepmother. He had a shotgun in his pickup, and this morning he'd put a pistol under the seat. He wasn't taking any chances—he'd already done that last night.

Sheriff McCall Crawford looked up to find a young woman standing in front of her desk.

"There wasn't anyone out front," the teenager said, looking nervous. She was slightly built, though tall and regal in appearance. Her straight shoulder-length hair was white blond, her eyes a clear, disarming blue. She had a pretty face that belied how young she really was, since on closer inspection McCall realized she was no more than a girl, probably not even out of high school.

"Can I help you?" McCall asked the girl.

"*You're* the sheriff?" She glanced at the open door and the name stenciled on it. "I thought the sheriff's name was Winchester?"

"I recently got married." It had been more than a year and a half, but McCall was wondering why she'd bothered to change her name, since everyone in town still called her Sheriff Winchester. "Why don't you have a seat and tell me what seems to be the problem."

"It's my aunt, Aggie Wells," the girl said as she pulled up one of the orange plastic chairs across from McCall's desk and sat down. "She's missing."

"How long has she been missing?"

"Several weeks now."

Several weeks? "Why have you waited this long to report her missing, Miss...? I'm sorry, I didn't catch your name."

"Cindy Ross. My aunt is gone a lot with her job. But this time she didn't call or come home."

"Where is home?"

"Phoenix, Arizona. That's where I live with my father."

"And your aunt?"

"She stays with us when she's in town. Like I said, she travels a lot but she calls me every few days from wherever she is and always calls on Sunday."

"So you haven't heard from her since..."

"The second week of May, that Sunday. She called to say she would be flying home that afternoon."

"Called from...?"

"Here. Whitehorse. She said she was driving to Billings, leaving her rental car and would be coming in on the last flight. I was to pick her up but she wasn't on the plane."

"And there has been no word?"

"No. My dad said something must have come up with her job." The girl looked down in her lap. "But when I called her office, they said she'd been fired a long time ago." She looked up, tears in her eyes. "I'm afraid something has happened to her."

"What does your father think?" The girl met her gaze, but didn't respond. "He doesn't know you're here, does he?"

"He says Aggie can take care of herself and that she'll turn up. But I have a bad feeling…"

McCall didn't like the sound of any of this. She picked up her pen. "Your aunt's name is Aggie Wells?"

"Agatha, but she's always gone by Aggie. She's an insurance investigator. That is, she was."

"What was she doing in Whitehorse?"

"She said she was trying to prove that some man murdered all three of his wives."

McCall's head shot up from taking notes.

The girl nodded knowingly. "I thought you might know about the cases. The man's name is Hoyt Chisholm. Aggie told me that he killed his first three wives and now he has married again. Her last appointment was with him and his new wife. She said they'd invited her out to their house for supper."

McCall was unable to hide her surprise. Everyone in town knew about the deaths of Hoyt's first two wives, and the disappearance of the third one.

The recent scuttlebutt throughout the county was about his new wife. McCall had heard that some residents were taking odds over at Whitehorse Café, betting how long this wife would be alive.

"My aunt told me that if anything happened to her, I was to make sure that Hoyt Chisholm didn't get away with another murder." The girl burst into tears. "I know he killed her."

BILLIE RAE FOUND HERSELF enjoying more than the ride to Havre. Tanner pointed out landmarks and told her stories. She knew he was trying to keep her entertained, to distract her from thinking about her life and Duane.

But the one thing she couldn't stop thinking about, sitting this close to Tanner, was last night. He had been so tender, so heartbreakingly sweet. She had cried after they'd made love.

"What is it?" Tanner had asked, sounding stricken.

How could she tell him that she felt she'd ruined her life by marrying Duane? That she'd lost her chance to be with someone like Tanner. Duane was going to kill her. Or at the very least, have her living in fear and on the run the rest of her life.

She could never be with Tanner again. As it was, she feared she had already put him and his family in danger.

"I forgot what happiness feels like," she had finally choked out. He'd held her and she'd spooned against him, relishing the warmth of his body and the way this man made her feel, dreading when the sun would come up and she would have to leave him.

"That's the town of Wagner down there," Tanner said now, pointing at the few buildings left. It appeared most of the towns along the Hi-Line were shrinking, some little more than a sign and a couple of old buildings.

"Butch Cassidy and the Sundance Kid held up a train not far from here," he said. "It was allegedly their last robbery before they headed to South America."

The day had dawned clear blue, sunny and warm. The land was a brilliant spring-green and, with the windows down, the air blowing in smelled of summer. It was the kind of day she remembered from when she was a girl and still had her illusions about life.

Billie Rae breathed in the sweet scents, catching a hint of Tanner's masculine one. When she was with him, she felt her strength coming back. Duane had done his best to beat it out of her. She was almost surprised that she could feel like her old self. But Tanner reminded her of who she'd been. Who she could be again—except for Duane who was determined to kill every ounce of independence in her.

She tried not to think about where he was or what he was doing. She knew he would be furious wherever he was. Just as she knew he would be frantically looking for her and wouldn't stop until he found her.

She shuddered at the thought.

"Warm enough?" Tanner asked, noticing.

"Someone just walked over my grave." She regretted the quick retort immediately. "You know what I mean."

"I do," he said and quickly pointed out an old Spanish mission on the road ahead. She was glad he didn't mention Duane, but neither of them had forgotten about him, she knew. She'd caught Tanner checking the rearview mirror occasionally—just as she had been doing in the side mirror.

Duane would not give up. She just had to make sure he never found her—or learned that Tanner Chisholm had been the one who'd saved her last night.

Hopefully Duane would also never learn about this trip to Havre. She hated involving Tanner Chisholm in the mess she'd made of her life any more than she already had. But she needed to sell the rings. Hopefully she could get enough to buy an old car and enough gas to put a whole lot more distance between herself and Duane before she found a job.

"You're going to have to deal with him, you know," Tanner said as if realizing she hadn't been listening about the old mission they'd just passed.

Billie Rae nodded. "I'm sorry. I just can't help thinking about him."

"How long have you been married?"

"Six months. We met in Oklahoma, where I was teaching kindergarten. Right after we eloped, Duane sprung it on me that he'd gotten a job in Williston, North Dakota, and we had to move at once. I didn't even get to finish the school year."

"You had friends in Oklahoma?"

She nodded. "I lost track of them once we got to North Dakota. Duane made sure of that. It's hard to accept that I'm the classic case. The abused wife. But Duane wasn't like this when we were dating. He was..." She let her voice trail off. "That's not true. The signs were there. He was controlling but I wanted to believe it was because he cared and just wanted what was best for me, like he said." She laughed at that. "I was such a fool."

"We've all been fools," Tanner said. "Myself included. But you realized your mistake and got away from him."

If only it were that simple.

"You don't know my husb...Duane," she said. She couldn't bear to call him her husband anymore. She hadn't only left him, hadn't merely taken off her wedding rings. In her heart she was no longer Duane Rasmussen's wife, and last night with Tanner she'd felt like a free woman, even though she'd only been kidding herself.

Under the law, she was still Duane Rasmussen's wife. Only technically, she thought, because there was no love in her heart for him. When had she stopped loving him? She didn't know. Just as she didn't know when she'd begun to hate him.

"He's...dangerous," she said, thinking that was putting it mildly.

Tanner let out a dismissive sound. "Only to a woman who can't fight back."

She shook her head. "He carries a gun, he kills people." And when he caught her, she wouldn't be the first person he killed in a rage. "Duane's a cop."

Chapter Four

It hadn't taken long for Sheriff McCall Crawford to verify what Cindy Ross had told her. Agatha "Aggie" Wells hadn't used her plane ticket—nor had she returned her rental car—a white SUV. Aggie had also been fired from the insurance company seven years ago.

"Can I be honest with you, Sheriff?" Wells's supervisor asked.

"Please."

"Aggie was one of our best. She was relentless. But something happened with this Chisholm case. Once she found out another of his other wives had died and a third had disappeared, she became obsessed. I'm afraid that for her the case became almost...well, personal."

"Personal in what way?"

The supervisor cleared his throat. "I know

this is going to sound crazy, but at one point I thought she had fallen in love with Hoyt Chisholm. See what I mean? Crazy, huh? It made no sense. If she really believed he'd killed his first two wives for the insurance money, and possibly the third wife who disappeared, then she wouldn't fall for the guy, right?"

McCall knew that crazier things had happened.

"Aggie just got so worked up when she talked about him, and even when she was pulled off the case, she continued to work on it in her spare time. Now, that's...scary."

Yes, McCall thought. And possibly dangerous.

"I take it she was never able to find any evidence that Mr. Chisholm had anything to do with the deaths or disappearance of his wives?" she asked.

"No evidence at all. Maybe that's what drove her so crazy. I finally had to let her go. May I ask why you're inquiring about her?"

"Apparently she hasn't given up on proving that Mr. Chisholm's guilty," McCall said. "She was in Whitehorse a couple of weeks ago and she met with the Chisholms."

"Chisholms?"

"Mr. Chisholm has remarried." McCall heard the heavy silence on the other end of the line and felt her concern growing.

"I have to tell you, I am very disturbed she is still apparently looking into this, and now with a new wife…"

"If you know something—"

"I probably shouldn't have said as much as I have," the supervisor said, clearly backpedaling. "Like I said, it was just a feeling. Aggie took her job very seriously. Quite frankly, I think she might…no, never mind."

"If there is something else you need to tell me, please do. It's important that I know everything. The reason I called you is because Aggie Wells has disappeared. She had called her niece to pick her up at the airport the day after she had dinner with the Chisholms, but never arrived. Nor has she used her plane ticket or returned her rental car."

"Let me guess. Aggie told her niece that if anything happened to her to contact law enforcement because Hoyt Chisholm would have killed her, right?"

"Yes, as a matter of fact."

"She insisted the same memo be put in her employee file here," the supervisor said. "We all thought she was just being paranoid, but what if Aggie was right? What if Hoyt Chisholm killed his three other wives and now plans to kill the fourth one as well?"

THE RINGS BROUGHT LESS MONEY than Billie Rae had hoped.

"The diamond is flawed," one jeweler told her.

She had argued that Duane had told her how much he paid.

"I'm sorry but there isn't any way your husband paid that kind of money for this," the last pawn broker said handing back the ring.

Tanner had driven her to all of the jewelry stores and pawnshops in town. He had waited in his pickup while she'd gone inside, as she'd asked him to. For that she was thankful because the experience had been humiliating. They'd all told her the same thing.

Duane had lied about what he'd spent on the rings. She realized he'd probably picked them up from a pawnshop to begin with or gotten them from one of the criminal types he loved to intimidate. Duane enjoyed the benefits that came with being a cop—those being throwing his weight around and flashing his badge to get what he wanted.

"What will you give me for the rings?" she asked the owner of the last place in town. When he told her, she had nodded, fighting tears of both discouragement and anger. Duane had lied to her from day one.

She knew that shouldn't have come as a surprise, the way their married life had turned out. But by the time she pocketed the small amount of cash she could get for the rings, she no longer had any illusions about the man she'd married.

"You all right?" Tanner asked as she slid into the truck seat next to him.

She gave him the best smile she could muster.

He laughed. "Stupid question. Let's get some lunch. There's a great Chinese food place here in the mall. You like Chinese?"

She knew she shouldn't spend any more time with him. While she couldn't imagine how Duane could have somehow followed them to Havre, she knew the longer she was around Tanner, the more she was putting him in danger.

"You have to eat," he said as if seeing her hesitation.

She nodded, hating the thought of the time that would come when she would have to tell him goodbye. "And then can we see if we can find me a used vehicle?" she asked as he started the truck and pulled out into the traffic.

He glanced over at her, but said nothing.

They ate at the Chinese buffet, finishing up with the fried donuts. Tanner was amusing during their lunch, telling stories about growing up on the ranch with five brothers.

Billie Rae looked around the restaurant. It had been so long since she'd felt normal. Sitting across from Tanner, she was able to eat without her stomach knotting up in fear that she would say the wrong thing and ruin it. With Duane she was seldom able to finish a meal without him getting upset and upsetting her in return.

"I saw you looking at that guy over there," Duane would say under his breath.

"What guy? Duane—"

"If you do it again, I'm going to go over there and punch him in the face, you understand?"

Tears welled in her eyes now at the memory of those horrible nights they would leave a restaurant, her in tears and Duane becoming more worked up by the minute. Billie Rae had known what was going to happen long before they got home, and she was never wrong.

Tanner reached across the table and put his hand over hers. "Billie Rae?"

She swallowed and wiped at her eyes with her free hand. "I'm sorry."

"He can't find you here. He has no idea where you are."

She nodded. Tanner didn't remove his hand. She didn't, either. She loved the feel of his large, callused hands. In his long fingers she felt a wonderful strength that seemed to flow into her. She thought of those hands exploring her naked body last night and remembered that feeling of both pleasure and sadness.

Billie Rae knew she would forever ache for his touch. As she looked across the table at this wonderful cowboy, her regret was that she would never see him again after today, let alone make love with him again. It was a regret she thought she couldn't bear to live with.

She realized Tanner was waiting for her to say more. He actually wanted to hear what she was feeling? "I was just thinking how nice this is, having lunch with you."

"I was thinking the same thing," he said and squeezed her hand gently before letting go.

She felt that well of happiness that she'd experienced last night after they made love. She was happy. The word almost seemed alien to her because she hadn't let herself admit how unhappy she'd been for so long.

Billie Rae had gone into marriage believing it really was until death do you part. She just hadn't known that those words had a totally different meaning for the man she married.

"I love hearing the stories about you growing up on the ranch," she said.

"Where did you grow up?"

She told him about being an only child, her father dying when he was young and her mother raising her in a small house in Oklahoma City.

"My life was very dull compared to yours," she said. "I wish I'd had brothers who tried to talk me into jumping off the barn roof."

"Sure you do," he said with a laugh.

"So you're all adopted?" She loved listening to him talk about his big family. Billie Rae had always dreamed of a large family as a girl. She wanted the noise, the activity, the feeling at night of all of them under the same roof.

"Yep, Dad likes kids. He adopted three when his first wife was alive. When three more kids needed a home, he was right there to take us. He would have taken more if he'd had better luck with wives." Tanner seemed to realize what he'd said. He stammered, "What I meant was—"

"It's all right."

"No, you need to understand. Two of his wives died. Another…disappeared. Emma, well, he married her recently after being alone for years. He's had a rough time of it. But I've never seen him happier."

"You're trying to tell me there is life after marriage?"

"Yep. And there is no shame in getting it wrong—and getting out."

She smiled across the table at him. He had no idea how impossible Duane would make that. There was only one way she feared she would be leaving Duane and that, as he told her many times, would be in a body bag.

"Emma is wonderful," she said, refusing to let Duane ruin this lunch. "I'm happy for your father. If he is anything like you…" Billie Rae ducked her head, embarrassed because she'd again thought of lying in his arms last night. But talking to Tanner was so easy. She could be honest with him without fear that what she said would set him off.

This closeness she felt with this man both warmed—and frightened her. It was too tempting to take him up on his offer to stay at the ranch and try to handle the Duane problem through legal channels.

But Billie Rae had already tried that. Tanner didn't know what Duane was capable of. She did.

After lunch, they stopped at one of the few used car lots in town and Billie Rae realized quickly that she wasn't going to get much of a vehicle and still have gas money to leave town.

"You can't run far enough, if that's what you're thinking," Tanner said as they walked around the last lot. "Sometimes you have to draw a line in the sand and fight. Come back to the ranch with me. I'll help you. You'll be safe. You shouldn't have to do this alone. I promise. I won't let anything happen to you."

He reached over and took her hand, squeezing it gently, and she was reminded of last night when he had pulled her through the rodeo crowd and kept Duane from catching up to them.

Tanner pulled her to a stop and turned her to face him. "There is something I have to tell you. Last night when I saw you," he said as if he too had been remembering when they'd met. "You're going to think I'm crazy, but it was love at first sight. It wasn't that I saw this beautiful woman and fell in love. I felt this strong connection as if you were some missing part of me, and when I saw you it was like this jolt…" He stopped and looked embarrassed.

She cupped his strong jaw with her free hand and smiled as she looked into his eyes. "I don't think you're crazy. I felt it too."

"Then come back with me—"

"I can't. If you knew Duane you would understand. I have to go. I have no choice." Her heart ached at the thought of never seeing him again. But if she wanted to protect him, she *had* to leave. Whatever had happened between them, she couldn't put Tanner and his family in jeopardy any more than she already had because of her bad decision to marry Duane and then make a wild run across the Hi-Line.

"At least think about it?"

She'd nodded, but she knew she couldn't change her mind—even as much as she wanted to.

At the cheapest car lot, Billie Rae bought a small beat-up old car that seemed to run fine and got good gas mileage. She paid cash but the owner of the lot still needed her to fill out paperwork—all traceable when you have a cop on your tail.

"I'm going to need some identification," he

said as he pushed the papers across the desk toward her. "Your driver's license," he said when she gave him what he took for a blank look. "I need to make a copy of it."

"I lost my purse," she said.

"Then I can't sell you the car until I have—"

"Put the car in my name," Tanner said and placed a hand on Billie Rae's shoulder before she could stop him. "It's better that way," he said to her after the owner had gone to make copies of Tanner's driver's license. "Duane won't know, right?"

She nodded numbly, thinking this would make what she had to do all that more difficult. Tanner had saved her last night in more ways than she wanted to admit and now here he was saving a woman he didn't really know again.

Billie Rae said as much to him and he laughed.

"I feel as if I've always known you," he said, and she thought he might be right. Sometimes she caught him looking at her as if he could see into her soul.

They *had* connected last night at the rodeo. She'd felt it and yet even now she denied the feelings for so many reasons. How could she trust her emotions right now? She couldn't. Not to mention she was on the run from her husband.

But Billie Rae knew the real reason she had to ignore what she was feeling was because it scared her. Tanner was the man she'd dreamed of marrying. She'd loved being on the ranch with his family. It only made her feel worse about marrying Duane. She'd ruined her life and now the best she felt she could expect was to keep her husband from killing her.

"I can't go back with you to the ranch," she told Tanner as they walked out to the car she'd bought. "I won't put your family in any more danger than I already have. I got myself into this. I'll get myself out."

"Billie Rae—"

She put a finger to his lips and felt a frisson of pleasure course through her from just touching those lips. She shook her head, afraid of what she might say. Or worse, do. If only she could just lose herself in him again. To be in his arms…

He leaned in and kissed her, and it took all of her strength not to throw her arms around his neck and let him take her back to the ranch, back to a life she had only dreamed possible, where she was safe and loved.

"I wish there was something I could say or do to keep you from doing this," he said as he drew back. "But I wouldn't force you even if I could. If you ever need me, though…"

Billie Rae had to fight tears. "Thank you for everything."

He pulled her to him, hugging her quickly as he whispered, "Be safe, Billie Rae." He stepped back. "Chisholm ranch will always be here if you're ever passing through again."

She realized then that he'd known she wouldn't be going back to the ranch with him. As she drove away, she tried not to look back. When she did, though, she saw Tanner standing beside the ranch truck watching her.

The look on his face seemed to say he knew there was little chance he would see her again. At least not alive.

Chapter Five

Emma Chisholm looked up to see the sheriff's SUV pull into the yard. At first she thought it was her stepson Colton's fiancée, Deputy Halley Robinson, stopping by, but the woman who climbed out wasn't familiar.

Going to the front door, she pushed open the screen and stepped out onto the porch. She hadn't been locking the doors for almost a week now—not since she finally felt confident Aggie Wells wouldn't be coming back.

Emma had just started feeling safe again. She'd noticed that Hoyt, though, was keeping his distance as if he really believed there was a curse on him and that Emma was doomed to die as well.

She couldn't bear the thought that he might regret marrying her. They'd been so happy. She thought of Hoyt tempting her up into the hayloft of the barn and their lovemaking. They'd proven that age didn't matter when it came to love and desire. Emma ached for her husband and had been determined to be patient with him. Once he realized that Aggie Wells was gone and that there was no stupid curse…or worse, that she might think for a moment he had anything to do with his wives' deaths…

Now, though, Emma felt her heart drop as she saw that the woman was the local sheriff. She'd heard that Whitehorse had a woman sheriff, but she hadn't heard how young and beautiful she was.

"Good afternoon, Sheriff," she said brightly as the woman flashed her credentials.

"I'm Sheriff McCall Crawford. You must be Emma."

"I am." Emma took her hand, amused by the surprise she'd seen on the young woman's face. Apparently the sheriff had been expecting Hoyt's new wife to be a trophy wife—not a short, plump redhead.

"I'd like to talk to you. Is your husband home?"

"No." Emma felt the first inkling of real anxiety. "Is something wrong?"

"I just need to ask you a few questions. When do you expect Mr. Chisholm to return?"

"He's working on the other side of the ranch. I don't expect him until late tonight. You know summer, with all this daylight, the men work late."

Emma realized she was doing too much explaining, giving away just how nervous she was. "Won't you come in, Sheriff? As they say, coffee is always on at any decent rancher's house. Why don't you join me for a cup back in the kitchen?"

The sheriff followed her to the kitchen and took a seat at the table while Emma set about getting the coffee and dishing up some of her freshly baked oatmeal cake that was still warm.

"Mrs. Chisholm—"

"Please, call me Emma," she said as she placed a brimming mug of coffee and a plate of warm cake in front of the sheriff. "Cream, Sheriff?"

"No, thank you."

Emma sat down across the table from the sheriff and, lifting her mug of coffee, studied the woman through the steam as she tried to still her raging nerves. "Something tells me this isn't a social call."

"Actually, I'm looking for Aggie Wells."

She knew the sheriff was also looking for a reaction and hoped to give her one she wasn't expecting. "A delightful woman. We had her to supper a couple of weeks ago."

"I heard that."

"Oh? Aggie told you, then." So the woman hadn't left town as Emma had hoped. Then why hadn't they heard from her? Because Aggie had been waiting until she had enough evidence to involve the sheriff?

"No, actually, her niece mentioned it. Apparently Ms. Wells is missing."

Emma put down her mug very carefully. The feeling of finally being safe evaporated like sun-kissed dew on the morning grass. "I'm sorry to hear that."

"I was hoping you might have heard from her."

"No, but then I didn't expect to."

McCall raised a brow. "Your business was completed with Ms. Wells?"

Emma laughed and helped herself to the cake. "I wouldn't say we had business together. I'm sure you know that Aggie Wells used to work for an insurance company. Apparently once she started a case, she had a hard time quitting until she was completely satisfied."

"And was she finally satisfied?" the sheriff asked.

"I think she was." Emma took a bite of the cake, closed her eyes and let it melt in her mouth. "Mmm." She opened her eyes and chuckled. "Sorry, but I do love this cake when it is still warm."

"You baked it?" McCall asked, glancing around the kitchen. "You don't have help?"

"Oh, yes, but I can't stay out of the kitchen. I love to cook and bake. It's a flaw." She felt the sheriff studying her, no doubt wondering about her other flaws. "The cook won't come in until later. It's the housekeeper's day off."

"When was the last time you saw Aggie Wells?"

"The night she came here for supper,"

Emma said, her heart in her throat. The sheriff wouldn't be here unless something had happened to Aggie. She couldn't help but think about her first reaction to the woman. She'd thought they could have been friends under other circumstances.

"Did she say where she was going when she left your house?"

"No. But since we didn't hear from her again, we assumed she'd left town."

"Do you know where Ms. Wells was staying?"

"No. I met her for a drink, though, out at Sleeping Buffalo." Emma could see that the sheriff was taken aback by how forthcoming she was being.

"Did anyone see you there together?"

She studied the sheriff for a moment, wondering if she didn't believe her—or if she was just looking for someone who might know how to find Aggie Wells.

"Just the bartender. A female." She described the woman, and the sheriff nodded as if she knew her.

"Mind if I ask what you talked about?"

"She informed me of her suspicions concerning my husband."

McCall had been in the middle of sipping her coffee but quickly put it down. "You weren't aware of your husband's past before then?"

"No, actually. I hadn't cared. I knew he'd been married and that he'd lost several wives. I love my husband, Sheriff. I trust him and I know he couldn't kill anyone."

McCall had just gotten back to her office and was sitting at her desk when she looked up to find a large man standing in her doorway.

His expression quickly changed from a slight frown to a smile as she greeted him.

"Sheriff Crawford," he said, stepping forward to extend his hand. His handshake was a little too firm, his smile a little too bright.

McCall instantly didn't trust him.

"My name is Officer Duane Rasmussen." He flashed his badge.

"May I see that?" she asked as he started to put it away. She could tell he didn't like being questioned even for something like this as he slowly handed her his shield.

She studied it and handed it back. "What brings a police officer from Williston, North Dakota, to Whitehorse, Montana?"

"It's a delicate matter," the cop said as he closed the door, pulled out a chair and sat down without being invited to. He leaned toward her, the smile this time self-deprecating.

He was good looking in the way a lot of ex high school football players are. She took him for a college linebacker who'd managed to stay in good shape, probably through hours in a gym.

"I'm looking for someone," he said.

She waited, knowing that if this was a professional investigation he would have come through normal channels and she would already be aware of the suspect through a bulletin.

This cop was off the leash.

"This is embarrassing," he said and did his best to look bashful. "It's my wife. She's not well. I'm worried about her. She took off without even her purse."

"What makes you think she's in White-horse?"

"I found my pickup at the fairgrounds where she'd run out of gas."

McCall lifted a brow. "She didn't take her own car?"

Some of his smooth veneer fell away. "She doesn't have her own car. She doesn't like to drive."

Alarms were going off all over the place for McCall. She didn't like this guy, was suspicious of his entire story and could see that he knew it.

"I was just hoping that you might have heard something that would help me find her," he said, looking as if he wished he hadn't come by to talk to her.

"What is your wife's name?"

"Billie Rae Rasmussen. But she could be going by her maiden name, Johnson."

McCall nodded and took down the cop's name and his wife's. "I'm sorry. I haven't heard anything, but I will keep an eye out for your wife. I'm surprised, if you're that worried about her, that you haven't put out an APB on her."

"I was hoping that wouldn't be necessary since I don't want to upset her. I just want to get her help. We've been trying to have a baby. I'm afraid she went a little berserk after this last disappointment."

"I'll need a description of your wife."

He pulled her picture from his shirt pocket.

McCall looked at the studio shot of the woman standing next to the man sitting across from her. The woman was small and pretty with a wild mane of dark curly hair and warm brown eyes. The sheriff asked for a more detailed description, jotted it down and handed the photo back.

"You have a number I can reach you?" McCall asked.

He gave her his cell phone number. "My wife is in a very...fragile state. I hate the thought of her out there somewhere..."

McCall nodded, wondering about the pretty dark-haired young woman in the photograph he'd shown her. There'd been something in the woman's eyes....

He rose to his feet. She could tell he hadn't got whatever he'd come here for and doubted it was information about his wife. "Thanks for your time, Sheriff." He said the last word with just enough emphasis to let her know what he thought of a woman sheriff.

She watched him leave, worried about his wife. McCall had come across his type before. But in this one, she sensed fury below the surface. This was a dangerous man, and she suspected the wife knew it and that's why she'd run.

After Officer Duane Rasmussen left her office, McCall told her deputies to be on the lookout for Billie Rae Johnson Rasmussen.

Now she had two missing women—one of them the wife of a cop, the other an obsessed insurance investigator after a man she believed had committed three murders.

McCall was thinking about that when her phone rang. "Sheriff Crawford," she said distractedly.

"I just found that vehicle you put the alert out on, the white SUV rental the missing woman was driving," a local highway patrolman told her. "It's down in the trees beside the Milk River, about ten miles north of town on River Road."

The same road as the one that went to the Chisholm Cattle Company ranch.

"The driver's side door is standing open, the keys are still in the ignition and there's a purse, the contents spilled on the ground nearby," the officer was saying. "No sign of the occupant."

"I'll be right there," McCall said and headed for her patrol car.

BILLIE RAE FILLED UP the car with gas, bought a map of Montana and tried to anticipate what Duane would do once he realized she wasn't coming back to his dad's old pickup.

From Havre, she had few options. She couldn't head north to Canada. Even if Duane didn't have the border patrol looking for her, he could find out if she'd crossed. She could head southwest to Great Falls. Or she could keep going west across the Montana Hi-Line toward Glacier Park. Either way she chose would be two-lane blacktop for miles.

Nor could she catch a commercial flight even if she had the money until she reached a much larger city, which would be several hours away minimum.

She still wasn't sure what she was going to do until she reached the junction on the outskirts of Havre and found herself turning south toward Great Falls.

Billie Rae had to fight the feeling that no matter which way she went, Duane would find her and it would all end the same way. So why run at all? Why not just turn around and go back?

Just the thought of Tanner kept her going down the highway. For so long she'd devalued herself, thinking she deserved everything Duane was dishing out. But Tanner Chisholm had made her feel whole again.

She prayed that Duane would never learn that Tanner and his family had helped her. She'd actually considered leaving some kind of trail so Duane would follow her and leave them alone.

This made her laugh. Duane didn't need a trail of breadcrumbs to find her. He could get the help of any law enforcement department. That's if he couldn't find her himself.

When she glanced in the rearview mirror, her heart lodged in her throat. No need to leave a trail. Duane had already found her.

A large black car came racing up behind her. She couldn't see the driver's face behind the glare on the dark windshield, and the car was too close for her to see the license plate. But her thundering pulse told her it was Duane.

She turned back to her driving. With growing panic, she saw that she was partway off the highway and headed for the ditch. She swerved back into her lane and glanced back again.

The driver of the black car swerved around her, sitting on the horn as the car zoomed past. She caught only a glimpse of the irate woman behind the wheel.

Billie Rae tried to catch her breath. Her heart was pounding and she felt sick to her stomach. That *could* have been Duane.

But it hadn't been. She was still free. Still safe. But for how long?

As she drove through the wide-open country, finally picking up the Missouri River as it cut a deep path through the state, she knew she had to come up with a plan.

She'd go as far as she could on what little money she had, then she would find a job, get an apartment and work until she had enough money to move on.

The hardest part would be establishing a new identity. She needed a social security number to go with that new identity. Or a job where she was paid cash and no questions were asked.

But she was determined. Tanner Chisholm had shown her what her life could be like with a loving, caring man. She desperately wanted that. The thought made her ache because she knew there was only one Tanner Chisholm and she'd just left him.

As the miles whizzed past and no sign of Duane's large black car coming up fast behind her, she was almost starting to relax a little when the right back tire blew.

Chapter Six

Stopping by the local sheriff's office had been a mistake. Duane had expected some country sheriff who would sympathize with his dilemma. If he'd known Whitehorse had a female sheriff he wouldn't have bothered.

Bitches always stuck together.

He'd driven into Whitehorse, which was the closest town to the fairgrounds, so he assumed that was where Billie Rae had gone. One of the locals had to have given her a ride. It stuck in his craw that someone had helped her. Maybe a woman. He swore under his breath. More than likely, though, it had been a man—possibly that cowboy he'd seen with his wife at the rodeo.

Whitehorse had turned out to be one of those small Western towns that dotted the Hi-Line of Montana. The towns had sprung up when the railroad came through. Many of them, like Whitehorse, had a main drag of brick buildings facing the tracks. Apparently in Whitehorse, though, they'd recently had a fire, because there was a gaping hole between two of the buildings.

After talking to the sheriff, Duane knew he now had to find Billie Rae before the local law did. Billie Rae couldn't have gotten far—not without any money or wheels.

But someone had helped her. Where would she have spent the night? In a local church? Do-gooders often put up the poor, helpless sorts who arrived in town without a car or food or money.

He was counting on her still being in Whitehorse. Sure, someone would be nice enough to give her a ride that far, but no farther since the closest towns were Glasgow, an hour away to the east back toward Williston and North Dakota, and Havre, an hour-and-a-half away to the west. The only other option was Canada, about fifty miles to the north.

He couldn't see her heading back the way she'd come, toward North Dakota. If she'd

left town, she would either go north toward
Canada or west toward Glacier Park.

But he still thought she hadn't gotten that far
yet. Even if she'd talked someone into giving
her a ride, this was a small town. Somebody
would have seen her. All he had to do was ask
the right people.

TANNER HAD GOTTEN BACK from Havre too
late. By the time he'd reached the fairgrounds,
there was no sign of the old pickup Billie Rae
said she'd escaped from her husband in—nor
of the black Lincoln she'd said her husband
had been driving.

"I should have gone out there first thing
this morning," Tanner had told his brother
Marshall when he'd called him after leaving
the fairgrounds.

"That would have been a boneheaded thing
to do," Marshall said. "Didn't you say this guy
is a cop?"

Now back at the ranch, he found his family
sitting around the dining room table eating an
early supper. It was clear that Marshall had
told them what Tanner had been up to.

"The man's abusing his wife," he said,

angry at the reproach he saw not only in his father's gaze but in Emma's as well. "I saw her black eye and the bruise on her cheek, but more than that, I saw her fear. Last night she was running for her life."

"Then she should have gone to the sheriff," his father said.

Tanner shook his head. "It would be her cop husband's word against hers. Even if he was arrested, he would get out on bail and be even more dangerous than he is now." Billie Rae was afraid of law enforcement and he could understand why, given she was married to a cop. "I tried to get her to stay. I told her I would help her," he said voicing his frustration.

"This woman really got to you, didn't she?" Emma said.

"I can't explain it. I saw her last night and..." He realized what he was saying and shut up. Emma, he suspected, would understand, but not his brothers. Unless anyone had felt something like that.…

"She wasn't ready for your help," Emma said. "There really is nothing you can do until she's ready."

"But Billie Rae wants out. Otherwise, why would she have run when he told her he would kill her if she did?"

Hoyt shook his head. "Most of the time, the woman goes back. Better the devil you know than the devil you don't. A smart man never gets in the middle of a domestic dispute, especially for a woman he doesn't really know."

"Tanner is no smart man," Marshall joked. "He's determined to save this woman—even from herself."

"You aren't going looking for this husband again, are you?" his father asked.

"I drove out to the fairgrounds when I got back from Havre, but he wasn't there," Tanner said.

"I told him it was a stupid thing to do," Marshall said and shrugged when Tanner sent him a withering look.

"She's afraid he's going to kill her," Tanner said. "He threatened to if she left him and she did. She needs help. Why can't you see that?"

"We do see it," Emma said. "But she didn't want yours or she would have stayed."

"She's afraid she put us all in jeopardy by letting me bring her here last night," Tanner said.

"Son, by now she could be headed back to her husband, for all you know," Hoyt said. "You can't save a woman who doesn't want to be saved. I ought to know."

Tanner knew his father was talking about his third wife, Krystal. He'd saved her from an abusive situation, only to have her disappear shortly after they were wed.

"Did Krystal go back to her abusive boyfriend?" Tanner asked, ignoring his brother's warning look not to.

"Yeah, she did and he was only her boyfriend. This woman you think you rescued is *married*. Let it go, son," his father said, laying a protective hand on his shoulder as he got up from the table. "We've got fence posts to set before it gets dark. Come on, work is the best medicine for what's ailing you. That, too, I know from experience."

"Your father only wants to help. He's worried about you," Emma said after the others had gone outside. "But Tanner, trust what you feel and pray. She's going to need it."

SHERIFF MCCALL CRAWFORD found the patrolman waiting for her at the spot along the Milk River where he'd discovered Aggie Wells's rental vehicle.

As she walked toward the stand of cottonwoods where the white SUV had been abandoned, there was no doubt in her mind that whoever had left it there had been trying to hide it. Law enforcement had been looking for Aggie's vehicle since the niece had reported her aunt missing.

She felt her heart beat a little faster as she neared the officer and saw his expression. "You found a body?"

He quickly shook his head. "But it appears we might be dealing with foul play. There is blood on the driver's seat." He handed her a flashlight so she could look into the tree-shaded vehicle.

She shone the beam into the rental, quickly taking in what appeared to be blood on the driver's seat; two open suitcases in the back, with clothes strewn around; a purse on the ground, the contents dumped as if someone had gone through her belongings. Or had hoped to make this look like a robbery.

"Have you checked the area yet?" she asked the patrolman.

"Just the immediate area."

McCall looked into the deep shadows under the cottonwoods. She could see the gleam of the river's dark surface through the low branches. The water looked murky. She felt a sudden chill as she remembered watching her father's pickup being pulled from an old stock pond where it had been buried in the mud for twenty-seven years.

At least whoever had hidden this car hadn't opted to sink it in the river where it might not have been found for years—or ever.

That thought gave her pause. Why hadn't the last person to drive this car done exactly that? Because they'd wanted the car to be found?

She glanced around. Maybe the person had been in a hurry. Possibly someone had been waiting for them up on the road, so they hadn't taken the time to do more than try to hide the car.

Too many possibilities, McCall thought. "Let's call in some help and broaden our search, and if we don't find her we're going to have to drag the river for her body."

As she reached for her phone, the question was still the same one she'd been asking herself since the niece had walked into her office. Where was Aggie Wells?

DUANE DECIDED THAT HIS best approach when he questioned the good people of White-horse, Montana, wasn't to admit that Billie Rae was his uncontrollable wife on the lam. That might garner unwanted sympathy for Billie Rae from the kind of people who took in strays and just felt the need to do good all the time—like whoever had given her a ride last night after the rodeo, the someone who just didn't know any better.

So it made sense that his best approach was to make her a dangerous felon and to flash his badge and put enough pressure on this town that someone came up with some answers. He figured if he moved fast, the local female sheriff wouldn't get wind of it.

He began to hit the churches, which were notorious for taking in stranded motorists and people passing through town. There were a half dozen in the small town, more churches than bars. When he struck out there he tried the motels, thinking the good Samaritan had put her up in one for the night.

Striking out again, Duane was tired and hungry and losing his patience. He considered repeating the story he'd told the local sheriff to some of his friends in law enforcement. If he put an all-points bulletin out on Billie Rae, everyone in the northwest would be looking for her. With luck, some good ol' boy would find her and—

With a start he realized that Sheriff McCall Crawford could have already done that. Someone could have already found his wife. But then, wouldn't the sheriff have called him? Probably not, he thought with a curse. Not until she talked to Billie Rae herself.

Duane realized it was time to put in a call to a couple of buddies he'd met who worked for the Montana state highway patrol department. They were good ol' boys. He gave them the same story he'd told the sheriff. It didn't matter if they believed it or not. They'd see that he got his wife back.

Then he found a small café on the edge of

town and ordered a cheeseburger, fries and a chocolate milkshake for a late lunch, telling himself it would be his word against his wife's. After all, he was a cop. And Billie Rae was…just his wife.

As he ate, he listened to the locals talking. He'd found you could learn a lot about a community by listening to the old guys talk in the local café. There was always a table or two of them and Whitehorse was no different. The talk was about range, cattle, water, weather and finally the rodeo.

Duane finished his meal, pushed the plate away and rose to go over to the table. "Gentlemen, sorry to bother you, but I heard you mention the rodeo." He took out his badge, flashed it and quickly put it away. He didn't need any smart rancher telling him he had no jurisdiction here. "I'm looking for a dangerous felon whose pickup was found at the rodeo last night. I was hoping you might have seen her."

"Her?" one of the old-timers said with a snort. Another one of them laughed as Duane handed him the photo he'd removed from his pocket of Billie Rae.

"You say this woman is a dangerous felon?" the man asked, disbelieving.

"The sweeter they look, often the more dangerous they are," Duane said, thinking how true that was. This woman was going to be the death of him, he thought.

"What's she wanted for?" another man at the table asked as the photo was passed to him.

"She killed her three children, ages eleven months, two and four years," Duane said without batting an eye. "Drowned them in the bathtub. The four-year-old fought for his life."

The men at the table wagged their heads in shock and horror, and quickly passed the photo back to him, wanting nothing to do with such a woman.

"I was hoping you might have seen her," Duane said solemnly. "As far as I can figure, she caught a ride with someone from the fairgrounds into town."

The waitress had come up beside him. She'd obviously been listening. He let her steal a look at Billie Rae's photo before he put it back in his shirt pocket.

"Rachel might have seen her," the waitress said and hollered at the cook to come out. "She was telling me about some woman she saw right as the fireworks were over."

Duane felt a surge of hope as a heavyset cook came out of the back. He showed her the snapshot of Billie Rae.

"I can't say for positive," Rachel said, handing the photo back. "But I think it might be her."

Duane had been a cop long enough to know that often people liked to be a part of the drama by saying they saw something they didn't.

"Where did you see her?" he asked.

"By the grandstands."

"There must have been a lot of people there last night," Duane said. "What was it about her that made her stand out in your memory?"

She seemed to think for a moment. "I guess the reason I noticed her was because she was going the wrong way. We were all trying to leave and she was heading back in as if she'd lost something, you know."

"She looked upset?" he said.

The cook nodded. "She was crying. I thought

maybe she'd misplaced one of her kids or something, and I was about to ask her if I could help, when I saw she already had help."

Duane felt his stomach roil. "She was with someone?"

"One of Hoyt Chisholm's sons."

Chapter Seven

Billie Rae gripped the steering wheel as the car rocked, the flat tire flopping loudly on the pavement as she tried to keep control of it. She finally got it pulled over to the side of the road and climbed out to see how much damage had been done.

There hadn't been a lot of traffic along the two-lane, but now several semis passed blowing up a cloud of dust and dirt. Covering her eyes, she waited until they passed before she opened the trunk.

A motor home blew past as she looked in the trunk for what she would need to change the tire. She'd changed a tire once, but it had been a long time ago. Since Duane didn't let her drive and had sold her car right after they got married—

It made her angry how she'd let him make

all the decisions in her life since they got married. But she'd learned early on not to argue with him. It was just easier—and safer—to go along with whatever he wanted than to argue, which always led to a fight.

She heard another vehicle coming and braced herself as she pulled out the bag of tools and waited for a truck pulling a trailer to roar past. Tanner, bless his heart, had made sure she had tools and the spare had air and some tread on it.

As she reached for the spare, she heard the sound of a vehicle slowing, then pulling up behind her. She turned to see a man in uniform climb out of a Montana highway patrol car.

ONE OF HOYT CHISHOLM'S SONS? Turned out there were six of them and they were grown men anywhere from their late twenties to their early thirties, and all six had been adopted by some big rancher to the north of Whitehorse.

Duane had gotten the information from the group gathered in the café.

"So what's the story on the Chisholms?" Duane had asked.

The waitress, not surprisingly, had turned out to be the most talkative. She told him about Hoyt Chisholm's four wives, two dead, one missing and one a newlywed, then about the six adopted sons.

"So you think he killed the other three wives?" he'd asked, not really giving a damn. All he really cared about was finding one of the man's sons—the bastard who'd apparently taken his wife away from the fairgrounds last night.

"There's this insurance investigator who thinks he did. Now she's up and disappeared. I heard they found her car by the river." She lowered her voice. "My good friend works as a dispatcher at the sheriff's department."

Great. "So all six of his sons live on this big, old ranch of his?" he asked, trying to keep the woman on the subject he *was* interested in.

"Nah, I think they've all moved out. He keeps buying up ranches and the sons move into the houses that come with them."

"This guy must have money."

"Insurance money from those three wives," the waitress said under her breath. "Everyone is wondering how long it will be before he kills the fourth wife."

"So which one of them was at the rodeo last night with the woman I'm after?" he asked the cook, whom he had talked into sitting down at a booth with him and the waitress since the place was dead right now.

"It didn't really register when I saw him with her," Rachel said. "I was mostly looking at her. But later…" she added quickly as she must have seen him getting upset. "As we were driving out, we passed the Chisholm Cattle Company ranch truck and I noticed there were three people in the cab." She looked a little uncomfortable and Duane tried not to show how frustrated he was getting.

"I was still wondering if the woman had found her child or if she was upset about something else," the cook said.

Duane nodded, wishing to hell she would get on with it, but knowing better than to push her again.

"I saw the woman was sitting in the middle and Marshall Chisholm was driving. There was another brother riding shotgun, but I didn't get a good look at him before my husband went flying around them." She realized she'd just told a cop that her husband had been speeding. "He slowed down after that, but Marshall had already turned off, so I didn't see them again."

"You wouldn't happen to know where Marshall Chisholm lives, do you?"

Duane tipped the cook and the waitress more than either deserved and left with directions to Marshall Chisholm's house. Apparently it was a good distance from any other ranch house and miles north of town.

The perfect place to hide a woman who didn't want to be found.

BILLIE RAE WAS SURPRISED Duane hadn't called the law on her sooner, she thought as she watched the highway patrolman get out of his car. He'd always told her not to bother calling the cops on him because they all stuck together.

She'd learned that the hard way the one time she'd tried to get help from the police.

But how had he known what she was driving? The car was in Tanner's name. Unless...

Her heart began to pound harder. She felt faint at the thought that Duane had found Tanner and what he had done to him to make Tanner talk.

The patrolman was a big man with an angular face. He wore mirrored shades and touched his nightstick as he walked up to her, his face stern.

She leaned against the back of the car, her legs suddenly weak as water.

"Looks like you could use a little help," the officer said and picked up the bag of tools from the ground where she'd laid them. "Why don't you get off the road and I'll take care of this. Won't take but a few minutes."

Billy Rae licked her dry lips, her mouth like cotton. "Thank you," she said, choking out the words.

She stepped off the road as he went to work on the tire. He was right, it didn't take him long. She'd watched him, telling herself this was all there was to him stopping. Duane hadn't put the word out on her. She had nothing to fear.

But as she watched the highway patrolman she was suddenly aware of how little traffic there was on the highway. She was alone out here in the middle of nowhere with a man in uniform—and she had learned not to trust a badge of any kind.

The highway patrolman put the blown tire in the trunk along with the tools and slammed the lid shut. "There, you should be fine now. I'd suggest, though, that you get that tire fixed or buy another one. Where are you headed?"

"Great Falls." It was the only town she could remember on the map.

"Good, it's not far up the highway. I'll follow you to make sure you don't have any more trouble."

"That's not necessary, really." She was trying hard not to let him see how upset his suggestion made her. The last thing she wanted to do was make him suspicious.

"It's not a problem," he said. "I'm headed that way, anyway."

All she could do was nod and thank him again.

Climbing behind the wheel, it took her a

few moments to get the car started, her hands were shaking so badly. He hadn't asked for her driver's license. Because he knew who she was, knew she didn't have it with her?

Billie Rae drove across the high bench for what seemed forever, the highway patrolman a couple of car lengths behind her. Finally the highway dropped down to the river and into the city of Great Falls. She pulled into the first gas station she came to and put down her window to let in fresh air as she tried to breathe.

What happened now? Would the patrolman detain her until Duane got here? She didn't think the man would hurt her, because he'd had the perfect opportunity out in the middle of nowhere if that's what he had planned.

When she looked, she saw the highway patrolman give her a friendly wave, turn around and leave.

Billie Rae couldn't believe it. Her relief was so intense, she had to fight tears. Was it possible Duane hadn't put the word out on her? He'd always told her he had friends all over the country and that there was nowhere she could hide from him.

"Can I help you?"

Startled, she jumped and turned to find a young gas station attendant standing next to her open car window. It took a moment before she could speak. "I blew a tire. I was hoping—"

"Pop your trunk and I'll take a look at your tire." A moment later, the young man came back to the window carrying the tire. "You picked up a nail. I can patch it. Shouldn't take long."

She heard a cell phone ring.

The attendant looked at her as it rang again. "I think that's yours," he said as he took the flat tire and headed for one of the bays in the garage. On the third ring, she realized the sound was coming from inside the glove box of her car.

As she opened it, she saw the cell phone lying inside. For just an instant she had the crazy, insane suspicion that Duane had put it there. Or the highway patrolman when she wasn't looking. But that was impossible. Only one person could have put it there, she realized as she snatched up the phone.

"Hello?"

"I see you found the phone," Tanner Chisholm said. "Look, I'm sorry. I was worried about you. You wouldn't take my other offers but I thought at least you'd have a phone if you needed it."

She was so touched that for a moment she couldn't speak. "Thank you."

"Where are you?"

"Great Falls. I had a flat, or I would have been a lot farther down the road."

He was quiet for a moment. "I wish you'd stayed. It's not too late to change your mind."

She wished she could. She remembered the views from the ranch, the feeling of peace and solitude and freedom. She remembered what it felt like to be in Tanner's strong arms, to sit at the table with some of his family and feel safe.

The attendant came back out with her tire and loaded it into the trunk.

"I should go," she said.

"I bought another cell phone. You have the number now since I called you. Be careful and, when you get to where you're going, give me a call if you want to."

"I will," she promised and snapped the

phone shut. As she started to put it back in the glove box, she saw the money Tanner had left for her and felt tears burn her eyes.

EMMA HAD BEEN EXPECTING the sheriff since the moment she'd heard about Aggie Wells's white SUV being found abandoned down by the river. The news had traveled like wildfire on the Whitehorse grapevine, not that Emma was on it since she was apparently too new in town, but Hoyt's ranch housekeeper had heard the news.

The moment she'd seen Mae Sutter's face when she'd come to work late that afternoon, Emma had known there was fresh gossip about the Chisholms.

"Spill it," she'd said to Mae, who'd looked surprised. But Emma was tired of beating around the bush with the cook and house-keeper. She'd tried to get close to them for weeks and they'd held her off as if she had a communicable disease.

Mae was a tiny thing. Emma had thought that a good gust of wind would blow the woman away. But Mae had turned out to be a lot stronger and more solid than she looked. She was also a good worker.

"I don't know what you're—"

"Save your breath, Mae. What's happened? And don't give me that innocent look of yours," she said to the housekeeper.

Mae straightened to her full height, all of five feet with her sturdy work shoes on, and tried to look indignant, but Emma could tell she was dying to tell everyone she knew— even her boss—who was involved.

"That woman who had dinner here the other night—"

"Aggie Wells," Emma said, trying to keep the tremor out of her voice. "What about her?"

"The sheriff questioned me about her," Mae said.

No surprise there. Emma put her hands on her hips and gave the housekeeper an impatient look, knowing there was a whole lot more to it than that.

"They found her car abandoned by the river," Mae blurted out. "There was blood on the driver's seat. They're dragging the river for her body."

Emma had always been proud of her iron-clad composure, but she felt all the blood drain from her face and had to sit down.

Mae got her a glass of cold water. "Are you all right?"

She nodded, knowing that Mae must be champing at the bit to tell everyone in the county about her reaction. Emma didn't care right now. "I liked Aggie," she said, tears in her eyes as she grasped the housekeeper's hand. "I know it sounds crazy, but I really liked her. I hope nothing happened to her."

Mae didn't look convinced. Nor was Mae surprised any more than Emma was when a few minutes later the sheriff drove up in the yard.

"I'll take care of this," Emma said, pulling herself together as she went to open the screen door and step out on the porch.

"Good afternoon, Sheriff," she said as McCall climbed out of her patrol SUV. "I thought we'd sit out here and talk, if that's all right. Would you like coffee or lemonade?"

The sheriff shook her head. "I need to speak with your husband."

Emma hadn't mentioned to Hoyt the sheriff's

earlier visit when he and his sons had surprised her and come home for lunch. She hadn't wanted to upset him. She told the sheriff what she'd told her before. Hoyt wasn't expected back until late.

"You've heard," the sheriff said as she studied Emma still standing at the top of the steps.

Emma nodded, not up to playing games. She was still shaking inside and felt light-headed. "Have you found her?"

"No, not yet. When you hear from your husband, would you tell him to contact me as soon as possible?"

"Of course." She didn't need to ask why. Of course Hoyt would be the number one suspect, with her falling in at a close second.

The sheriff seemed to hesitate. "Did either of you leave the house that night after supper with Agatha Wells?"

"No. We were here the rest of the night." But she knew that wouldn't clear them. Hoyt had gotten up early the next morning and left. Emma didn't know where he'd gone, had just assumed it had something to do with the ranch.

She, herself, had gone into town that morning and didn't have an alibi for her whereabouts as she had taken a ride south to the Little Rockies to clear her head. The truth was, she hadn't wanted to stay around the house. She'd been too antsy, afraid of what Aggie Wells would do next.

When Aggie had left, her last words had been a warning that Hoyt Chisholm was dangerous, that he'd killed all three of his former wives and that Emma would be next.

Emma had hoped that having Aggie out to dinner would change her mind about Hoyt. It had been a foolish idea. At dinner Aggie had seemed to enjoy Hoyt's company, but later she was more convinced that Emma was living with a killer.

"Are you sure you wouldn't like some coffee or lemonade?" Emma asked the sheriff, hating the fear she heard in her voice.

"Thank you, but I need to get going," the sheriff said, turning to leave. "Do you know where your husband is working today on the ranch?"

Emma didn't. Hoyt had said they were putting in a new fence, but she had no idea where.

He hadn't confided in her much about the ranch and his work lately. She'd told herself he had a lot on his mind, just as she told herself he hadn't been avoiding her. The thought that she'd been lying to herself about a lot of things scared her more than she wanted to admit.

After all this had come out about the deaths of two of his wives and the disappearance of the third, he had begged her to leave him. She had refused. It was after that that Hoyt had made himself scarce, as if he feared just being around her might put her in mortal danger.

"I assume you already tried to reach him by cell phone," Emma said.

The sheriff nodded. "It went straight to voice mail. I left him a message. It's important I speak with him as soon as possible."

"I'll tell him. And you'll let me know what you find out about Aggie?" Emma called from the porch.

The sheriff had reached her patrol SUV. She glanced back at her and nodded.

What was Emma thinking? If Aggie's body was found, she and Hoyt could expect to see the sheriff at their door—probably with an arrest warrant for at least one of them.

DUANE FOUND Marshall Chisholm's farmhouse without any trouble. It was off the county road, back in a quarter mile and sheltered by a large stand of old cottonwoods.

He drove up to the two-story house, noting there were no vehicles parked in front. The large old barn out back had a tractor and some rusted farm equipment around it but nothing inside. The perfect place to hide a vehicle.

He pulled his car into the back of the barn deep in the shadows, then taking the tire iron from the back, went to have a look in the house. While he didn't believe Marshall was home, he couldn't be sure Billie Rae wasn't hiding inside.

He was only a little surprised to find the back door unlocked. People in this part of Montana were awful trusting. Duane let himself in.

The kitchen linoleum was worn and dated just like the appliances and cabinets, but everything was clean. Duane couldn't imagine living alone and wondered about a man who could. No wonder the man had jumped at the chance to pick up a woman like Billie Rae.

The living room was neat as well, even though the furniture was also dated. It would seem that the son, even an adopted son, of a rich rancher could afford better furniture.

He climbed the stairs to find two bedrooms, one empty, the other with an antique metal bed frame and antique dressers that had probably come with the house.

Duane moved to the bed, pulled back the quilt and smelled the sheets. Billie Rae hadn't slept here. In the bathroom, he also found no sign that Billie Rae had ever been there.

Maybe she hadn't spent the night here, but Marshall Chisholm still had to know where Billy Rae had gone last night after he'd given her a ride to Whitehorse.

Duane settled in to wait for Marshall Chisholm to come home.

"ANY NEWS?" MCCALL ASKED when she reached her husband. As a local game warden, Luke Crawford was often involved with any law enforcement in the county. Since he'd been in the area checking fishing licenses and had a boat, he was now involved in the search for Agatha Wells's body.

"Nothing so far. We're dragging the river."

"I just spoke with Emma Chisholm again. After she and her husband, Hoyt, had Aggie out to supper the night she disappeared, Emma says neither of them left the house after that."

"You believe her?"

The sheriff thought about the new Mrs. Chisholm. She liked her and wanted to believe her. "Not sure. She's scared, which makes me think her husband wasn't in the house all of that time."

"From what you told me," Luke said, "Hoyt Chisholm has the most to gain by this woman's death."

"I spoke with the insurance company that Agatha Wells worked for. She was fired. Her boss said she became obsessed with the Chisholm case, convinced that Hoyt killed all three of his wives, including the third one who disappeared. I found out that he only recently had her declared dead."

"And now he's remarried. Wouldn't that

explain the fear you saw in Emma Chisholm? I know that would scare me if your last three husbands met with accidents or just plain disappeared."

McCall chuckled. "I scare you already."

"True." She heard the soft, seductive tone in his voice and felt a small shiver. Could she love this man anymore? Not likely.

"I just needed to hear your voice," she said truthfully.

"Always glad to oblige. See you later?"

"Absolutely." She disconnected, and following a feeling she hadn't been able to shake all day, she put out an all-points bulletin on Billie Rae Johnson Rasmussen.

By the time Billie Rae got something to eat from a fast-food place, filled the car up with gas and looked at a map to decide which way to go next, it was getting dark.

The emotional roller coaster of the past forty-eight hours had taken its toll on her. She felt wrung out and knew she wasn't up to driving much farther. The next large town was hours down the road and she didn't trust staying in the smaller Montana towns, feeling it would be too easy for Duane to find her.

She could almost feel him breathing down her neck. He wouldn't give up. It wasn't in his nature—not when he would feel justified for whatever he did to her. He would be driven and nothing and no one could stop him.

At least Great Falls was large enough that she should be able to find a motel, pay cash and get some sleep with some assurance she would be safe. At least for tonight.

She thought about changing her appearance, bleaching her dark hair, cutting it, getting a pair of glasses at the dime store. Instead, she picked up a baseball cap at a convenience store and stuffed her long hair up under it.

When she found a motel downtown, though, she ran into the same thing she had when she purchased the car. No identification.

"I'm sorry, we need a credit card or some kind of identification," the older male clerk behind the desk told her.

"My purse was stolen," Billie Rae said. "I'm just trying to get home."

"Where's home?"

"Spokane." She picked the name out of thin air.

The clerk studied her. She was still wearing the blouse and slacks she'd been wearing when she'd made the run for it. She must look a mess. Tomorrow she had to buy some more clothing. Thanks to Tanner, she could afford a few items.

Billie Rae also realized that her "disguise" had been a mistake and quickly took off her baseball cap. Her long curly dark hair spilled around her shoulders.

Duane had told her she looked too young, that she should try to look older; people thought he'd robbed the cradle worse than he had. As it was, he was seven years her senior—him nearly forty.

She knew it bothered him, turning forty, and that was part of the problem. While he had begun to gray around the temples, Billie Rae could still pass for her early twenties, although she tried to dress and act older to please Duane.

"Well, I suppose it will be all right this time," the clerk said now.

She started to fill out the registration card

as he watched her. She was so nervous she wrote down her first name without thinking, then unable to quickly think of a second name, wrote down Chisholm. After all, the car was registered to Tanner Chisholm.

"Billie Rae Chisholm," the man said reading the card. She'd done better on making up an address in Spokane, Washington, but didn't dare make up the zip code.

"You don't know your zip code?"

"I keep forgetting it. We just moved there."

He nodded and put the registration card away as if he didn't believe anything she said but no longer cared. He gave her the key and told her how to get to her room.

By the time she reached the motel room, she was trembling all over and furious with herself. If Duane started calling motels in Great Falls, he would have no trouble finding her since she'd already made the clerk suspicious.

She thought about just leaving, hitting the road, trying to drive to another town or even another motel in Great Falls. But it would be the same thing all over again. Exhaustion overtook her. She plopped down on the bed, telling herself she would only rest for a few minutes before leaving, and fell into the sleep of the dead.

DUANE SAW THE LIGHTS coming up the road. One vehicle. Good, Marshall Chisholm was alone. Unless he'd brought a girlfriend, but Duane was pretty sure that wasn't the case or he wouldn't have picked up Billy Rae last night.

He smiled when he saw the cowboy climb out of his truck alone. Duane loved being right.

Marshall Chisholm was good sized. Duane wasn't all that sure he could beat him in a fair fight, but then there was no chance of that.

He waited until Chisholm opened the door and stepped in before hitting him from behind, knocking him to his knees.

The idea was to disarm him—not to knock him out. While he'd love to beat the hell out of the man who'd interfered in his marriage, he needed to know where Billie Rae was first.

"What the hell?" the dazed cowboy said when Duane stepped in front of him.

"Where is Billie Rae?"

The cowboy was on his feet before Duane could get a good swing with the tire iron. The blow didn't even stun him. Marshall Chisholm grabbed the tire iron before Duane could hit him again.

Seeing how this was going down, Duane pulled the gun just so the cowboy knew who was boss here. "Where is my wife?"

Marshall Chisholm took a step back at the sight of the gun. He rubbed a hand over his jaw, and his eyes widened just enough that Duane knew they were finally on the same page.

"Now you *remember?*" he said with a laugh. "Where is she?"

"You're the cop," Marshall said as if trying to get up to speed. Or maybe he was just re-minding himself that he'd just slugged an of-ficer of the law.

"That's right," Duane said, brandishing the gun. "And you're the son of a bitch who picked up my wife last night at the rodeo." He took a threatening step toward Marshall. "Now put down the tire iron and tell me what you did with her and where she is now." He fired a shot next to the cowboy's head. Wood splintered, the boom echoing through the house. "I suggest you start talking."

Chapter Eight

Tanner woke to an unfamiliar sound. It took him a moment to realize it was his landline ringing. After he'd put his cell phone in Billie Rae's car, he'd picked up another cell phone and had his number changed, but no one but Billie Rae had the number.

He'd slept badly last night and now felt groggy as he glanced at the clock. It wasn't even daylight yet.

As he reached for the phone, he realized it might be Billie Rae calling. He knew he shouldn't have called her yesterday evening, but he'd needed to hear her voice, needed to know she was all right, needed to be sure she hadn't changed her mind and gone back to her abusive husband. He'd also wanted to make sure she found the phone—and the money—he'd left her.

"Hello?" He heard the hope in his voice that it was Billie Rae and that she'd changed her mind and was coming back. He should have known that no call this time of the morning was going to be good news.

"Son, it's Dad."

"What's wrong?" Tanner sat up, now fully awake. Had Hoyt heard something about Billie Rae? Was that why he was calling?

"It's your brother Marshall. He's in the hospital."

"What happened?" All Tanner could think was a car accident.

"He's been beaten up pretty badly, but the doctor says he's going to be all right. He's asking to see you."

Beaten up? How could he have gotten into a *fight?* Last night Marshall said he was heading home after they finished work late, that he was tired and going home to his house.

"He asked to see all of the family?" Tanner asked in alarm. Maybe his father was wrong and Marshall was worse off than they thought.

"Just you."

Thirty minutes later, Tanner found his

brother sitting on a gurney in the emergency room of the hospital, Hoyt and Emma standing nearby. Marshall's head was bandaged and he had a dark row of stitches along his jaw.

When he saw Tanner, he asked their father and stepmother to give them a moment alone.

"Come on, Emma," Hoyt said, shooting Tanner a look that spoke volumes. He was responsible for this?

With a curse he realized who had done this to his brother. "I'll kill the son of a bitch," Tanner swore again, seeing red. He'd gotten in the middle of Billie Rae's marriage to a cop, of all things, and now he had gotten his brother almost killed. How could this situation be any worse?

Marshall shook his head. "I'm fine. But we have to find Billie Rae before he does."

The anger fled in an instant at the sound of her name, leaving him clearheaded. "You told him where she'd gone," Tanner said, no judgment in his tone. His brother had taken a beating because of him.

"Not on your life. I sent him north to the

Canadian border to buy us time," Marshall said, sliding off the gurney.

"Sir, the doctor hasn't released you," the nurse said, rushing toward them. "He wants to keep you overnight. You have a concussion."

"She's right," Tanner said, putting a hand on his brother's arm. "I can handle this."

Marshall met his gaze as though assessing if he thought his brother was too emotionally involved, then he slumped back against the gurney.

"I'm so sorry," Tanner said as he and the nurse helped Marshall back up onto the gurney.

"This isn't your fault. I know what would have happened to Billie Rae if we hadn't helped her last night and so do you, but he's a cop, little brother. You can't kill a cop, even a bad one, and if you tangle with him you'll get yourself killed."

"I can handle this."

His brother shook his head. "Even when he pulled the gun on me, I wanted to go for the bastard's throat. I'm afraid that's exactly what you would have done and he would have killed you. I'm telling you, Tanner, this dude is dangerous. Just make sure he doesn't find Billie Rae until you can get her some kind of protection from this psychopath."

SHERIFF MCCALL CRAWFORD got the call before breakfast. Luke had left early since he was overseeing the dragging of the river. She had wanted to go with him but got held up with a phone call.

She had just hung up when the phone rang again. It was her deputy.

"We just found a grave not far from where Aggie Wells's car was abandoned by the Milk River," he said. "It's not our missing vic, though," he added. "These remains have been here for a lot longer than a few weeks."

By the time McCall reached the scene, Coroner George Murphy was crouched beside an open hole in the side of the riverbank.

"Looks like whoever killed her dug into the side of the bank, shoved the tarp-wrapped body in, then let the soft dirt slide down and cover her." He motioned to the bones lying on what was left of an old canvas tarp.

"Her?" McCall asked.

"Definitely a woman. I'd say in her late twenties."

McCall glanced at the gaping hole in the side of the bank. "How was it again that you found the grave?" She remembered finding her father's. It had been like opening Pandora's box and she suspected this grave would be no different.

"Apparently another dirt slide unearthed it—or maybe one of the searchers inadvertently did," the coroner said. "This morning I happened to spot a bone and a piece of the tarp sticking out."

"That was handy, wasn't it?" she said, never comfortable with coincidence. "Or maybe someone wanted us to find it. Any chance of matching dental records?"

"She's had some dental done," George said slowly, then met her gaze. "I think you might get luckier with her medical records. She had an abnormal amount of broken bones for a woman her age."

"Are you suggesting some medical reason for that?" McCall asked.

"Maybe. More than likely this woman was

seriously abused in her twenties, I would say."

"You can tell all that from her skeleton?"

"It's the type of breaks. Facial, wrists, arms, ribs…" George looked a little green around the gills. He always did when things got ugly. For a man who didn't like knowing about the evil things humans did to one another, it was amazing the EMT was still willing to act as the county coroner.

"How long would you estimate that the remains have been there?"

George sighed. "Hard to say, but given the amount of decomposition…I'd guess, and remember this is just a guess, twenty-five years. Maybe less, maybe more." He launched into a speech about all the factors that made a body deteriorate, a speech she'd heard many times before.

"Let's get her ID'd as quickly as possible," McCall said and glanced through the trees where she could see Aggie Wells's vehicle. The wrecker was coming today to take it to the sheriff department's storage unit as evidence.

They'd been searching for Aggie Wells's

body and now another woman's had turned up? And still no sign of Aggie.

McCall didn't like what she was thinking and was surprised when the very person she was thinking about called.

"Sheriff Crawford here," she said into the phone. She listened as Hoyt Chisholm told her why she needed to come down to the hospital, then said, "I'll be right there."

DUANE SAT IN HIS CAR down the street from the small town hospital. He knew Marshall would warn whoever had been in the pickup that night with Billie Rae after the rodeo. All he had to do was wait and see who showed up.

Duane wasn't surprised at all when a cowboy drove up shortly after the father and stepmother had arrived. He recognized him from the high school yearbooks he'd found at the library.

Tanner was a big cowboy like his brother, but as Duane had always said, "The bigger they are, the harder they fall." And this one was going down.

He smiled to himself as he waited for a

few minutes to see if anyone else would show up. When no one did, he climbed out of his car and walked down the deserted street to the pickup the brother had arrived in. It had Chisholm Cattle Company printed on the side, Duane noted as he slipped under it and secured the tracking device.

Another benefit of being a cop, he was able to get all the toys that went with the job, along with anything else he wanted from the sleaze-bags he came in contact with on the streets.

Slipping out from under the pickup, he moseyed back to his car and checked it on his cell phone. "Modern technology," he said in admiration, pleased with himself, as he looked at the small screen. Now wherever Tanner Chisholm went Duane was sure to follow, and he had no doubt that this cowboy was going to lead him straight to Billie Rae.

"It's just a matter of time now, Billie Rae," he said to himself, then swore as he spotted a sheriff's department vehicle coming up the street. He slid down in his seat, swearing profusely as the patrol car pulled into the hospital parking lot.

He'd told Marshall Chisholm not to call the

law or he would come back and finish him. Apparently the hick hadn't taken his threat seriously. Duane rubbed his jaw where the cowboy had got in a good punch. First Marshall had lied to him about where Billie Rae had gone. Duane had believed that under the threat of death the cowboy had told him the truth. But one call to the border after he'd left Marshall and he'd verified that Billie Rae hadn't been anywhere near the crossing.

Duane told himself he should have known better than to believe that she'd head for Canada. Billie Rae was proving she wasn't as stupid as he'd once thought. Obviously she'd known how easily he could find out if she'd crossed into Canada, so she'd probably gone in another direction. What he needed to know, though, was *which* direction—and how she was getting wherever the hell she thought she was going.

These Chisholm cowboys had been playing him. They really had no idea what a mistake that was yet. But they would soon.

As he watched the woman sheriff being met at the door by the parents of Marshall Chisholm, Duane knew it was time to get out of town. Apparently that was what Billie Rae had already done.

Wherever she was, he was counting on Tanner Chisholm leading him right to her.

TANNER CALLED BILLIE RAE the moment he left his brother's hospital room. The cell phone rang four times. A shaft of icy fear made his stomach roil at the thought that she'd dumped the cell phone, afraid her husband would somehow be able to follow her because of it.

Billie Rae answered on the fifth ring.

"It's Tanner. Are you all right?"

"What's wrong?" She sounded as if she'd been asleep. He'd forgotten how early in the morning it was.

"Tell me where you are."

"No, I—"

"Duane beat up my brother Marshall. He's in the hospital."

"Oh, no." He heard what sounded like her crying softly. "Is he all right?"

"He'll live but he's worried about you. He sent me to find you and make sure you were safe until something can be done about your situation." Tanner could hear her moving around.

"If Duane found out your brother was with us that night at the rodeo, then…oh, Tanner, he'll come after you next. He won't stop with your brother. You're in terrible danger. The rest of your family might be as well."

"You just worry about yourself right now."

Billie Rae let out a choked laugh. "I'm the one who put your brother in the hospital, the one who has put you all in danger."

"Listen to me, Billie Rae. None of this is your fault."

"You're the one who said I needed to draw a line in the sand."

"That was before I saw what Duane did to my brother."

"He's capable of doing much worse. But you were right the first time, I can't keep running. He will go after anyone who helps me."

"My brother has filed charges against him," Tanner said. "The only place he's going is jail."

"No, you don't understand. Even if the sheriff finds him and arrests him, he'll be out within hours and even more furious. Tell your brother not to press charges."

"Billie Rae, it's too late. If you come back to Whitehorse—"

"And what? Get a restraining order against Duane?" She let out a humorless laugh. "Do you really think that would do any good? Tanner, I know about battered women whose husbands threaten to kill them. The husbands find a way to get to them no matter what and do exactly what they said they would."

Tanner wanted to argue, but he'd seen too many examples of women in the news who'd been killed by their husbands or boyfriends—or lived in fear of them even with their abusers behind bars.

"Then I will get you enough money so that you can disappear and Duane will never be able to find you," he said even as he realized it would mean he would never see her again, either. The thought hurt. But all that mattered right now was keeping her safe.

"Tanner, do you really think there is that much money in the world?" she asked. "Even if I could accept your too generous offer, I can't live like that, always looking over my shoulder. This was the reason I hadn't tried to leave Duane before. And now I've gotten your brother hurt—"

"He's going to be all right. He told Duane you were headed for the border in one of our old trucks."

She groaned. "Once he finds out that your brother lied to him—"

"He isn't going after my brother again. The sheriff is putting a deputy outside his room until he is released. There is an APB out on Duane. Everyone will be looking for him. I'm betting he will get out of Whitehorse and not come back. It's you I'm worried about. Come back to the ranch. I'll make sure he never hurts you again."

"Tanner..." she said with a sigh.

"I know. You don't even know me."

"That's the amazing part. I feel as if I have always known you. This closeness I feel..." Her voice broke off.

"I feel the same way. I can't explain what happened the moment I saw you, but I don't want to let you go."

"And I can't let him hurt you or your family simply because you helped me."

Tanner heard something in her voice that scared him. "You can't go back to him. You know it will be worse for you. That's if he doesn't end up killing you. You can't go back because of me. Please, I can't let that happen."

"I can't run, either. You were right. I have to take a stand."

"*No,* I was wrong. Billie Rae—"

"Make sure you and your family are safe."

"My father and brothers will see to that. Billie Rae, I'm leaving right now headed for Great Falls. Meet me halfway between Whitehorse and Great Falls. There's an Indian casino called Northern Winds just outside of Havre. I'll be waiting for you in the parking lot." He heard her open the motel room door; he could hear traffic outside. He knew he was losing her. "And if you're still determined to go back to him after we talk, then—"

"Thank you, Tanner. I wish we'd met under different circumstances."

"Billie Rae. Billie Rae?" The line had gone dead. He called back but it went straight to voice mail.

Swearing, he started his pickup. If she was headed back this way, then he would see her on the highway. He would do whatever he had to do to stop her. He couldn't let her go back to that madman because of him.

All he could hope was that after she hit the road on the way back that she would change her mind and meet him at the casino. He said a silent prayer that she would be waiting for him when he reached Northern Winds as he pulled away from the Whitehorse hospital and headed west.

Tanner hadn't gone far when he checked his rearview mirror. He couldn't take the chance that Duane was still in town, waiting for him to lead him to Billie Rae.

But there were no other vehicles behind him as he turned onto Highway 2 and headed west toward Great Falls. Wherever Duane Rasmussen was, he wasn't behind him. Breathing a sigh of relief, Tanner settled in for the long drive, thinking about Billie Rae and fate and how he was going to stop her.

BILLIE RAE COULDN'T BREATHE. Wasn't this what she'd feared? She choked back a sob and closed the motel room door behind her. She'd never felt such pain—not even when Duane had hit her. The woman she'd been—before Duane Rasmussen—never dreamed she would find herself in this position.

Her heart ached and she felt sick to her stomach. She'd only made it worse by making love with Tanner the night before. What if Duane found out? She told herself there was no way that would ever happen. But they hadn't used protection. Last night she'd told herself it wouldn't matter. Duane was going to find her and kill her before she'd even know if she was pregnant.

But what if she was? She touched her stomach. Just the thought of having Tanner's child sent a wave of excitement through her. Then instant regret that she had now possibly endangered yet another life. What was she going to do?

You should never have left me. This is on your head. You forced me to hurt someone else. You deserve everything you're going to get.

She slid behind the wheel of the car and sat, trying to pull herself together. Since she'd realized the mistake she'd made marrying Duane, Billie Rae had been desperate to get out—but she hadn't known what to do. Duane had made it clear that leaving him was out of the question. The fact that he was a cop made it all the more impossible.

She'd felt trapped with no way out and no one to turn to. Early on in their marriage, she'd had a friend she'd met at the small market within walking distance of their home. The friend had noticed Billie Rae's bruises and had tried to help her.

Not long after that, the friend had suddenly moved away without a word.

Billie Rae had inquired about her through a mutual acquaintance at the market and found out that a policeman had come around the night before her friend had left. Duane. After that Billie Rae hadn't let anyone get close, knowing the price they would have to pay if Duane found out.

Now she had involved the Chisholm family and it had gotten Marshall injured. She didn't want to think about what Duane would do to Tanner if he knew how much he'd helped her. And yet Tanner hadn't backed down for a moment. He was still ready to help her—even knowing now what Duane was capable of.

She felt such a well of emotion at the thought. Tanner was the kind of man Duane would call a fool. Duane would scoff at anything that smacked of chivalry. No doubt because he could never measure up and he knew it. That was why he resented men like Tanner Chisholm so much.

Thinking of Tanner reminded her of his smile, the warmth in his brown eyes, that spark that had brought the old Billie Rae back to life when he touched her. Tanner had already saved her in ways he couldn't imagine. But she couldn't let him get in any deeper.

After a few minutes, she could breathe again. She picked up the map, remembering something she'd noticed on it yesterday. It was a dangerous plan. A desperate plan. But for the first time in months, she felt she was finally thinking clearly. She almost felt like her old self—the strong, independent woman Duane had done his best to destroy.

For so long she thought she deserved what she got because she was the one who'd married Duane. *You made your bed, now lie in it,* her mother used to say.

No more. Anger boiled up from deep inside her. No more. She *didn't* deserve this. Nor did the Chisholms who had helped her. Tanner had been right. It was time to draw a line in the sand and fight.

It was time she took her life back.

Or lose it.

But at least she wouldn't go down without a fight, and if she was lucky she'd take Duane with her. Taking a deep breath, she braced herself, opened her phone and tapped in his number. Her hand was barely shaking as the phone at the other end began to ring.

"Hello?" He hadn't recognized the cell number. Tanner had blocked the ID on it. She could hear Duane's car stereo in the background and wondered where he was. He turned down the music and repeated, "Hello? Who is this?"

Just the sound of his voice brought it all back. Fear knifed through her, and for a moment her courage faltered. She drew on the memory of the woman she had been in Tanner's arms, the woman Tanner Chisholm had seen in her, the woman he was bound and determined to save even if it meant risking his own life.

"It's me," she said.

The soft chuckle that came over the line sent a chill through her. "I wondered when I'd be hearing from you." Duane's words were clipped. Anyone else might not have heard the fury behind them. But she heard it and, if she hadn't known before, she knew now that he would beat her to death this time if she gave him a chance.

Terror gripped her and she couldn't breathe, couldn't speak, couldn't think for a moment. Then she reminded herself that Duane had been systematically killing her for months. He'd tried to suffocate her in a loveless marriage, beat her down, make her question herself, especially her strengths, and he'd hurt her in more ways than she wanted to admit.

"So you're ready to come home." His tone made it clear he couldn't wait to get his hands on her.

And that was exactly what she was depending on.

Chapter Nine

As Emma and Hoyt left the hospital, she saw her husband stop to take a call on his cell phone. He turned his back to her and she felt her heart drop—just as it had weeks ago when she'd feared her husband was having an affair. Instead the woman who he had been talking to back then was Aggie Wells, the former insurance investigator determined to see Hoyt hang for murder.

Hoyt hadn't wanted her to know that Aggie was not only back in town—but also that she was more determined than ever to see him go to prison for murder.

"Who was that?" Emma asked now as he put his phone away and joined her. She was half afraid it was Aggie. And at the same time, almost hoping it was. No one wanted Aggie Wells to turn up alive more than her.

Hoyt hesitated, then sighed. She'd made him promise there would be no more secrets. She still felt guilty about that because she had things she'd never told her husband, things she wanted to hide as well.

"It was Tanner. He wanted to tell me he was going after Billie Rae."

"He's his father's son," she said, not at all surprised—even after what had happened to Marshall, or because of it, Tanner would be all the more determined to protect the woman.

"He's a fool," Hoyt said as he led the way to the ranch pickup. The doctor was keeping Marshall in the hospital for observation even though her stepson had only a minor concussion. She'd seen how upset her husband had been after their visit with Marshall in the hospital and knew he feared that another son would be injured—or dead—before this was over.

She noticed how Hoyt glanced around the hospital parking lot. He was looking for Billie Rae's husband—or at least anyone who might fit that bill since the only description they had of him was what Sheriff Crawford had given them.

"Tanner's worried the husband might come after us, isn't he?" Emma said as she climbed into the pickup next to Hoyt.

He shot her look. "The man sounds crazy. It is cause for concern since his wife involved us in her troubles."

"Hoyt," Emma snapped as he started the engine and headed toward the ranch. "How can you say such a thing? The poor woman was running for her life. The man is an animal. Can you imagine what he'll do to Billie Rae if he finds her?"

Hoyt swung his head around to look at her. "Can you imagine what he'll do to Tanner if he finds him with his wife? And what will have been the point? Women like that go back to the men who abuse them."

"Women like *what?*" Emma demanded, shocked by his last statement. She too was worried about Tanner. But she was also worried about Billie Rae. And her husband had hit a nerve. He didn't know she used to be one of those women. But like Billie Rae, she hadn't stayed—nor had she gone back in the way he meant, anyway.

"You know what I mean," he said. "I'm

worried about my boys and now Tanner is going after the woman."

"You raised your sons to help those in need. The only reason Billie Rae would go back to her husband is to protect your boys, who by the way, are men. Are you going to let that happen?"

"What would you like me to do?" Hoyt demanded.

"This attitude of yours is all because you're so certain that your third wife went back to her abusive boyfriend." He'd told her about Krystal, a woman he'd tried to help by foolishly marrying her.

"She *did* go back. I hired a private detective. Krystal went back because she missed the drama, especially the honeymoon period, after he's beaten her up, when he pleads for her forgiveness, treats her like she's rare crystal, buys her things, promises never to hurt her again until he does and the cycle starts all over again. She was hooked on it and life with me was just too damned dull for her."

All Emma heard was the part where Hoyt said he'd had proof that Krystal went back to her boyfriend. "You hired a private investigator who had proof and you didn't give that information to Aggie?"

He stared straight ahead, ignoring her as he drove.

"No, you didn't give Aggie the information because you wanted to save face, because of your damned male ego. You'd rather have people believe you're a murderer." She was furious with this man she'd come to love more than life.

"Aggie Wells already believed I killed at least one of my wives," Hoyt snapped. "What could another one hurt? Anyway, you wouldn't understand."

"Oh, I understand just fine, Hoyt Chisholm. If Aggie had known about any of this—"

"She would still believe I killed Krystal. Don't you get it? She would think I couldn't stand my wife leaving me and that I went after her and killed her. Maybe killed the boyfriend too because shortly after that, both of them disappeared and not even the private detective I hired could find them."

This news took the wind out of Emma's sails. Hoyt was right. He would still look guilty, maybe even guiltier than he had.

He glanced over at her. "I'm not as stupid as I look. After I calmed down, I told the P.I. to get proof that Krystal was alive to give to Aggie. I thought maybe then she'd believe that I didn't have anything to do with my first wife's drowning or Tasha's accident. But by then, both Krystal and her abusive boyfriend had vanished."

Emma fell silent as Hoyt turned onto the road to the ranch. "I'm sorry. You could have told me."

"I just did. It proves nothing." He reached over and took her hand, all the frustration leaving his voice. "This crazy cop husband aside, I'm still worried as hell about you. I'm so afraid something is going to happen to you."

"I'm fine as long as I'm with you."

He squeezed her hand. "How did I get so lucky as to find you? Maybe that's what scares me. I feel like I'm tempting fate."

"Don't be silly. I'm hard enough to get along with that maybe *I'm* your punishment."

He laughed softly, but didn't disagree.

"I saw the sheriff talking to you. What was that about?"

"She wanted to know the last time I saw Aggie Wells. If I knew where she'd been staying. If she happened to mention where she was going or what she was doing. The usual."

Emma realized he'd been questioned by the sheriff on numerous occasions before. But those times it had been about his wives. Her heart went out to him and for a moment, she hated Aggie Wells for making him have to relive this all over again.

"So you told her the last time you saw Aggie was that night at dinner?" Emma said.

He shot her a look. "Are you asking me when was the last time I saw her?"

"No, I—"

"I didn't kill her, if that's what you're asking."

"I know you didn't kill her. I just thought—"

"That I might have met her the next morning?" He shook his head. "I never saw her again after that night at dinner and I hope to hell I never see her again. Any more questions?"

Emma shook her head, wishing she'd kept her mouth shut, but that was so not like her.

Had she really believed Hoyt would meet Aggie the next morning?

"I have no idea where she is or what happened to her."

Emma could hear the fear in her husband's voice. It matched her own. Since Aggie's car had been found with, according to the scuttlebutt around town, her purse and suitcase, and blood on the driver's seat, the sheriff's department had been searching for her body along the riverbank.

"The sheriff asked where she could find me and I told her we were headed back to the ranch," Hoyt was saying. "I intend to stay with you until this cop who beat up Marshall is caught."

That sounded just fine with Emma. She'd missed her husband. Ahead she could see the main house at Chisholm Cattle Company. All Emma wanted to do was get home, go upstairs with her husband and make love. She said as much to Hoyt.

He swore under his breath. She thought that was his reply to her suggestion. Instead he was staring at the house as he pulled into the yard.

Emma turned to see that the front door was standing open, no other vehicles around and since Marshall's brothers, other than Tanner, were now all at the hospital...

"Stay in the pickup," Hoyt ordered as he pulled down the shotgun from the rack behind the pickup seat. Grabbing a handful of shells, he carefully closed the truck door and hurried toward the house and the open doorway.

Emma, who had never been good at taking orders, especially from a man, was hot on his heels. As she hurried up the steps and crossed the porch, she heard Hoyt moving cautiously through the rooms.

She would have followed him farther into the house, but she stopped just inside the door pole axed, her heart pounding as she breathed in the familiar scent of Aggie Wells's perfume.

The insurance investigator was no longer missing. She'd been in this house again, which meant she was alive even though her car had been found abandoned and the sheriff suspected foul play.

But it was the second realization that panicked Emma. Aggie Wells was still determined to prove Hoyt Chisholm a murderer—even if it was her own "murder" he went to prison for.

"BILLIE RAE?" There was now a sharp edge to Duane's voice.

"I'm still here," she said into the phone. She told herself to just breathe. She could do this.

"Right, and where exactly is *here?*" he asked as if she was a disobedient child. It was the same tone he'd used with her since she'd said, "I do."

"I'm broke down near a town called Fort Benton."

He swore. "Of course you are and now you need my help." There was smug satisfaction in his voice. She knew he was smiling and that, she'd learned, was when he was his most dangerous.

"How long will it take you to reach me?" she asked, needing to know where he was and how much time she had to prepare.

"I'm leaving Whitehorse now." She heard him put down his car window. A moment later a siren came on. He'd put the portable cruiser cherry light on the roof. "Give me the directions."

She told him how to get to the dead-end river road she'd seen on the map.

"How could you be so stupid as to go down a dead-end road?" he demanded, but didn't wait for an answer. "Never mind. The two to three hours you're going to have to wait for me will give you time to think about what you've done and how you intend to make it up to me." He hung up.

Billie Rae snapped the cell closed with trembling fingers, then went back inside the motel room for the phone book. She found the first address she needed, then checked the Great Falls map at the front and started the car.

She shuddered at the thought of facing Duane and feared she wouldn't have the courage to carry through with her plan. But she knew that if she showed any sign of weakness, she was a dead woman.

What sustained her was the knowledge that if she didn't make her plan work, Duane wouldn't end it there. He would still go after

Tanner. In his mind, Tanner would be to blame for all of this.

Pushing the thought away, she concentrated on what she had to do. Tanner would be waiting for her at Northern Winds casino. He should be safe there. Just thinking about him made her feel stronger as she drove to the first shop on her list.

SHERIFF MCCALL CRAWFORD was just leaving the hospital after putting out a warrant on Duane Rasmussen when her cell phone rang.

"We have a positive identification on the remains found buried out by the river," Coroner George Murphy said.

McCall braced herself because she had a bad feeling she already knew.

"The remains are those of Krystal Blake Chisholm," George said.

Hoyt Chisholm's third wife, the one who disappeared almost thirty years ago.

"Cause of death?" she asked.

"A blow to the back of the head, according to the crime lab doctor who did the autopsy.

It's all in the report, but I know you can never wait for the report, so I called you."

McCall smiled. "You know me too well. Thanks." Krystal Chisholm's murder cast a whole new light on the deaths of Hoyt Chisholm's other two wives who had died under questionable circumstances—and now insurance investigator Aggie Wells's disappearance.

"We found something among the remains in the tarp I think you're going to want to see," George said.

"I'll be right there."

As she walked into the autopsy room a few minutes later, she pulled on latex gloves and stepped over to where the box of weather-rotted scraps of canvas tarp and the remains had been placed on a gurney.

George handed McCall a piece of silver jewelry.

"The victim's?" she asked, wondering why he'd wanted her to see this.

He shook his head. "My best guess? It's part of a men's bolo tie." A lot of western-dressed men in this part of the country wore a bolo tie. It was as dressed up as they ever got. The tie consisted of two thin cords that formed a loop with the ends dangling down from some sort of decorative clasp that held the tie together.

"How would it have ended up with the body?" she asked just wanting his take on it. She already had her own theory.

"The killer has the woman down, she reaches up and grabs the bolo tie, the silver clasp slides off."

Her thought as well. "Wouldn't the silver be more tarnished, though, if it had been with the body for the past twenty-five to thirty years?"

"Silver reacts badly to just about everything, latex gloves, ammonia, chlorinated water, air pollution, perfumes, hair sprays, even some foods like onions and eggs, anything salty unless the silver is plated with a thin layer of metal protection, which older jewelry wasn't," George said and then seemed to notice her looking at him sideways. "My sister works for a jeweler."

"Sorry, as you were saying…"

"Humidity alone can cause silver to tarnish."

McCall nodded. "So who knows how tarnished it would be, is that what you're saying?"

"Something like that," George said. "What do you think of the design?"

While he was squeamish about the violence of murder and what it did to the human body, he seemed to be getting into the investigation part of his job a lot more than when he first started, she thought.

She'd been turning the piece of silver in her fingers. If you turned it one way it appeared to be three tiny silver horseshoes welded together.

If you turned it the other way, it looked like three small C's.

She held it up. "One of a kind, I'd say." She was waiting for George's opinion, which she knew he was dying to give her. "Probably someone had it specially made at a jewelry store. Could be tiny horseshoes or—"

"We both know that it is three C's and that

those three C's are for Chisholm Cattle Company," George said, losing his patience with her.

She laughed. "Why do I get the feeling you have something to back up that statement?" George was all about facts.

"In fact I do," he said stepping over to the laptop computer on a nearby desk, "I thought I'd seen Hoyt Chisholm wearing this very piece of jewelry and I was right."

McCall stepped over to look at a photograph of the cattleman taken at Whitehorse Days twenty-seven years before. Hoyt was wearing the bolo tie with the silver clasp, and he was with a woman. The cutline under the photo identified the woman as Krystal Chisholm.

DUANE HAD FORGOTTEN ABOUT Tanner Chisholm after Billie Rae's call. He'd been so excited at the prospect of getting to his wife that Tanner Chisholm had been the last thing on his mind.

That was, until he heard the soft beep from the tracking device on the seat next to him.

"What the hell?" he said as he saw Tanner's location. "The son of a bitch is following *me?*"

He almost ran off the road he was so busy staring at his cell phone screen. How was this possible? The cowboy had left Whitehorse before him. He must have stopped for gas or something. How else could Duane explain it?

Unless he was right and the bastard was actually *following* him.

All he had been thinking about after Billie Rae's call was getting to her. It was so like her to call—after she'd gotten herself into a pickle. Just the sound of her voice had gotten his blood boiling.

He chewed at his cheek for a moment now, giving this change of events some thought. Did he really give a damn about this cowboy? Wasn't getting to Billie Rae and settling this all he should concern himself with?

As anxious as he was to reach Billie Rae— there was always the possibility that she would get some wild idea to take off again—especially if someone encouraged her. He realized he couldn't let the cowboy follow him to her.

Another thought breezed past. What if Billie Rae had also called her cowboy savior, covering all her bets?

Duane swore. He was going to have to take care of Tanner. He watched the highway ahead looking for the perfect place to wait in ambush.

Chapter Ten

All it took was a couple of calls to jewelers in Glasgow and Havre. McCall hit paydirt on her second try.

"Chisholm, sure, I know him well," the elderly sounding jeweler said.

She described the clasp for the bolo tie.

"Yep, I made that, but not for Hoyt. It was an anniversary present I made for his wife to give to him," the jeweler said.

"His wife?"

"What was her name? Just a minute. I can look it up. I keep records back to when I started this business." She heard him digging in a file. A moment later he came back on the line. "Just as I remembered. An anniversary present, the clasp for the bolo tie and a set of cufflinks. Three tiny silver C's for Chisholm

Cattle Company. I made them for Krystal Chisholm, October 16, 1984."

Twenty-seven years ago. Just about the time that Hoyt had married Krystal, McCall thought.

She asked if the jeweler could fax her a copy of that order, thanked him and hung up.

Earlier at the hospital, Hoyt Chisholm had assured her he knew nothing about Aggie Wells's disappearance. He'd sworn he hadn't seen her since the night she'd come out to the ranch to have dinner.

But given what she knew now, she wondered how long it would be before they found her body as well.

McCall sat for a moment before she placed the call to the county attorney. It was time to bring in Hoyt Chisholm before another wife ended up dead.

"AGGIE WAS HERE," EMMA SAID when Hoyt returned to where his wife was still rooted just inside the door.

"There's no one in the house. The front door probably blew open," he said as if he didn't hear her. He started toward her to put his shotgun back into his pickup.

"Did you hear what I just said to you?" she demanded. "Aggie was in the house again."

He stopped in front of her and frowned. "Emma—"

"Didn't you smell her perfume when you entered the house?"

He looked at her, shook his head and swore under his breath. "Where are you going with this?"

Did he think she was making it up? Imagining it? "I know what I'm talking about. Don't you see what she's doing? She's trying to frame you for murder."

"She's been doing that for years," he said as he tried to step past Emma.

"Hoyt, I'm telling you she set this whole thing up, her disappearance, her car being found, the blood on the seat, the whole thing to make it look as if you killed her."

He shook his head. "I really don't want to talk about this." He pushed past her and headed for his truck.

"Hoyt Chisholm, do not treat me like I am imagining things," she said following him as far as the porch. "I smelled her perfume. She's been in our house again while we were gone. It's as if she knew we were all going to be at the hospital and—"

"And what, Emma?" he demanded as he turned from hanging up his shotgun on the rack behind the seats. He slammed the pickup door before he turned back to her. "Emma, why would she be sneaking around our house? For what possible reason?"

"She did it before."

"Yes, no doubt to let me know she hadn't given up sending me to prison." He swore under his breath. "Aggie Wells is the last person I'm concerned with right now."

"I smelled her perfume. She was in this house again." But she was talking to his back for he had turned and was headed out to the barn where he always went when he was upset—or didn't want to hear what she had to say.

As she started after him, Emma saw the sheriff's patrol car coming up the road toward the house.

TANNER KNEW HE WAS DRIVING too fast. He'd made good time. Even after his stop at the bank to get more money for Billie Rae and gas in the pickup in Havre, he was going to beat Billie Rae to the casino parking lot.

The casino wasn't far ahead. Just the thought of seeing Billie Rae again had his heart pounding with anticipation. He thought about the first time he'd laid eyes on her at the rodeo grounds.

He still couldn't describe the effect she'd had on him. Love at first sight? How was it possible to fall in love with a complete stranger in a nanosecond? It was easier to believe they'd been together in a past life and had found each other again in this one.

Whatever it had been, it had happened. In that instant, Billie Rae's face had lit up in a burst of fireworks and he'd felt his heart skyrocket. The fireworks had showered down from Montana's big night sky, the air smelling of summer and rodeo concession stand food. Music had played against the boom of the rockets exploding over their heads and he'd lost his heart.

That moment was frozen in time forever for him.

But as odd as it sounded, maybe it had been

luck that brought them together. That is, if they could stop this maniac after her.

Ahead, Tanner saw a large black car parked at the edge of the road. His heart lodged in his throat. Had Duane somehow found out where Billie Rae was going to meet him?

The black car pulled out, turned in his direction and headed down the highway toward him. Past it Tanner could see the casino in the distance. His gaze shifted from the black car approaching him to the casino parking lot.

He didn't see Billie Rae's small red car. He hoped that meant she hadn't arrived yet—and not that Duane had already stopped her.

His gaze shifted quickly back to the black car as it increased speed on the other side of the highway coming in his direction. The car was big and black, possibly a Lincoln like the one Duane drove, just as Billie Rae had described it and it was gaining speed quickly.

Tanner tried to see the face behind the steering wheel as it neared, but the sun was glinting off the windshield. He felt himself tense. He gripped the wheel tighter, bracing himself because he feared the driver of the black car was planning to swerve into his lane.

At the sped the car was coming, it would probably kill both of them if Tanner couldn't avoid the crash, but then Duane Rasmussen was a psychopath, wasn't he?

The car was within yards of him, still on the other side of the road. And then it was roaring by in a blur, throwing up dust and gravel on the edge of the highway. Tanner caught a glimpse of an elderly man behind the wheel with a shock of white hair as the car sped past.

Tanner had to hit his brakes to make the casino turnoff. As he fishtailed into the parking lot, his blood was still hammering in his ears. He'd been so sure the driver of the black car was Duane on a suicide mission that was going to take them both out.

Now as he brought the pickup to a stop in the parking lot, he had to take a minute to catch his breath. He glanced around the lot. Billie Rae wasn't here yet. He hoped that meant she was still safe. Police officer Duane Rasmussen was probably still back in White-horse. Or maybe already in jail.

Tanner tried to reassure himself that everything was going to be all right. Billie Rae would be here soon. He would talk her out of going anywhere near her husband. Somehow it had to work out because he couldn't bear the thought that he might never see her again. Or worse, that Duane would find her.

DUANE SWORE AS HE STARED at the GPS screen. Tanner Chisholm had been right behind him, then he suddenly stopped when Duane had found the perfect place to finish the bastard for good?

He tapped the screen on his cell phone and looked down the highway in the direction Tanner had been heading until a few minutes ago. No sign of a Chisholm Cattle Company pickup headed this way. Instead it appeared the pickup had left the highway and was no longer moving. Why would he pull off?

Duane looked at his watch. Turn back and find him? Or wait? Or keep going and take care of Billie Rae and then worry about Tanner Chisholm?

He tapped the screen again, thinking something was wrong with the tracking device. Maybe it had fallen off the cowboy's rig. The tiny icon representing the Chisholm Cattle Company pickup still hadn't moved. The location appeared to not be that far back up the highway.

What if Billie Rae's call had been bogus? What if she was meeting the cowboy back down the road? Duane tried to remember if there'd been a place back up the highway where Tanner and Billie Rae might have planned to meet.

With a jolt he remember seeing a large building set off the highway. A Native American casino.

Duane slammed the car into gear and, with tires throwing gravel, flipped the Lincoln around and headed back down the highway. If he was wrong about Billie Rae being with Tanner right now, he'd have to make this fast, which annoyed him to no end. He'd wanted to make the cowboy suffer enough that he wouldn't be stupid like his brother and call the law on him.

On impulse, Duane called the cell phone number Billie Rae had called him from this morning. It went straight to voice mail.

"What the hell?" he said tossing the phone on the passenger seat as he floored the Lincoln.

He was driving so fast he almost missed the turn into the casino. The Chisholm Cattle Company pickup was sitting in the lot away from the few other vehicles, the cab empty.

Duane hadn't taken Tanner Chisholm for a gambler, but then he'd gambled with his life when he'd helped Billie Rae, hadn't he?

Parking next to a large motorhome out of sight of the cowboy's pickup, he sat for a moment considering his options. He didn't have the patience to wait for Tanner to come out. He was too anxious to get to Billie Rae.

But then again, she might be inside the casino with the cowboy right now.

The problem was he would have to be careful once inside. If he made a scene, he could end up in a Native American jail cell. He got out of his car. He didn't think walking into the casino wearing his shoulder holster would be the smartest idea, either. While he didn't have jurisdiction in Montana, he really didn't on the reservation.

But he also wasn't going in the place

unarmed. He took off the holster, tossed it on the seat and removing the Glock, tucked the gun into the waistband of his slacks. The tail of his shirt covered it well enough. If this place was like most casinos, it would be fairly dark inside.

Duane locked his car and walked toward the front door, hoping he didn't find the cowboy and his wife together gambling when Billie Rae had convinced him he needed to save her at the end of some dead end road up the highway.

If that happened, Duane wasn't making any promises about what he would do. But as it happened, Duane didn't have to go inside the casino.

BILLIE RAE LOOKED AT the pile of supplies she'd put in the car trunk, glanced at her watch and slammed the lid. Fortunately she didn't have far to drive, she thought as she slid behind the wheel.

She repeated the mantra that had been echoing in her head since Tanner's call. *Desperate times called for desperate measures.* She wondered, though, if Duane rationalized his behavior with the same kind of catch phrases.

The cell phone rang on the seat where she'd laid it. She checked to see who was calling as she drove out of Great Falls. Tanner. She wanted to answer just to hear his voice and take some comfort in it. But there was nothing more to say. She let it go to voice mail. If he knew about her plan he would try to stop her.

She couldn't let that happen.

Billie Rae knew how dangerous her plan was. So much could go wrong she didn't want to think about it. But she felt she had no choice. She had to stop Duane from hurting anyone else and if that meant sacrificing herself in the process, then so be it.

Ahead she saw the sign for the dead-end road she'd seen on the map. Turning off the main highway, she drove down the narrow dirt road until it dropped precariously toward the river gorge below.

Billie Rae hit the brakes and sat for a moment gripping the steering wheel. Where was the road she'd seen on the map? What if it had washed out?

Setting the emergency brake, she climbed out of the car and walked to the edge. The wind whipped her hair around her face. She brushed it back and looked down. Her stomach knotted at what she saw. Far below was the river, a green snake of rock and rushing water.

The road she'd seen on the map was little more than a rocky two-rut path that had been cut into the side of the mountain high above the river gorge. Getting to it would require her to drive off this steep edge to reach it.

She couldn't do it. She took a step back, glanced at her watch. Time was running out. Duane would be here in the next thirty minutes, maybe sooner.

That's when she saw it. The swinging foot bridge across the narrow gorge. It was at the end of the road just like it had shown on the map. Billie Rae stared at it for a long moment, surprised that it was just as she'd envisioned it—except even from here, she could see it swinging in the wind.

This was pure suicide, she thought as she looked from the swinging footbridge high over the river gorge to the road that ended at the bridge. The map had failed to give her any idea of just how narrow or how rough the road was. Add to that the large sign that prohibited anyone from going past this point unless for authorized use only.

She'd always been so law-abiding she actually hesitated, then reminded herself given what she planned this was a pretty minor infraction.

Taking a deep breath, she eyed the road for a moment, then gathering her courage, she got back into the car, released the emergency brake and, riding her foot brake, let the car drop over the rim into the river gorge.

TANNER FELT AS IF HE'D suddenly been dropped in Las Vegas. From the carpet to the noise and flashing lights of the gambling machines, it took a moment to get his equilibrium once he'd stepped inside the casino.

The place was huge and nearly empty, which made the beeps and dings echo through the large room giving it an end-of-the-world feeling as he walked through.

He couldn't help searching for Billie Rae among the few patrons and employees even though he didn't think she could have been here yet unless like him, she'd driven too fast. He wasn't all that sure that she could get that kind of speed out of the car she'd purchased—not to mention the fact that her car hadn't been in the lot.

But to be safe, he found the rear exit and checked to see if there was a back lot. No Billie Rae.

He found the men's room on his way back through the casino. He kept telling himself that once he had a chance to talk some sense into Billie Rae, she would come back to the ranch with him.

Hell, maybe by now the sheriff had already picked up Duane. Even if she couldn't hold him long before the cop made bail, at least Duane wouldn't be stupid enough to get into any more trouble in Whitehorse.

As he walked back to his pickup to wait, Tanner hoped Billie Rae would be here soon. He couldn't wait to see her. He glanced down the highway in the direction of Great Falls looking for her small red car.

He was almost to his pickup when Duane Rasmussen came out from behind a van and jumped him.

EMMA COULDN'T LOOK AT HER husband for fear she would burst out crying. She had taken his hand the moment they'd all sat down at the kitchen table and now gripped it tightly, afraid of what would happen if she didn't hang on for dear life.

As she looked across the table at the sheriff, she told herself this wasn't happening. "Are you sure I can't get us some coffee? Maybe some of that cake…" Hoyt squeezed her hand making the rest of her words dissolve in her mouth.

"You're sure it's Krystal," Hoyt asked the sheriff. He hadn't seemed surprised when McCall had informed them that Krystal Blake Chisholm's remains had been found not far from the ranch.

Emma refused to read anything into that. Hoyt must have suspected his third wife was dead after she and her old boyfriend had both disappeared. But hadn't he said the old boy-friend lived down in Wyoming? So how did

Krystal end up buried up here? And where was the boyfriend?

Emma's mind whirled with such thoughts as she tried to concentrate on what the sheriff was saying.

"We have matched both dental records and the DNA which you provided when she disappeared," McCall said.

"So it really is her?" he repeated as if in a fog. He seemed to have aged right before Emma's eyes.

"Where did you find her?" Emma asked.

The sheriff seemed to hesitate, but she had to know the news would be all over the grapevine, if it wasn't already. "Near where we found Aggie Wells's vehicle." She was looking at Hoyt, obviously hoping for a reaction.

Emma sat up straighter. She'd erroneously thought the remains had been found on the ranch. Why else would the sheriff be acting as if she was about to arrest Hoyt at any moment?

"Near where you found Aggie Wells's car?" she repeated.

Didn't anyone else see what was going on here?

"You haven't found Aggie's body, though, have you," Emma challenged. Hoyt squeezed her hand. She pulled it free. "And you're not going to find it because Aggie isn't dead."

"Emma—"

It was the sheriff who cut Hoyt off. "Where would you suggest we look?" she asked, her eyes narrowing as she turned her attention on Emma.

"Aggie staged her disappearance," Emma said and Hoyt groaned next to her. "She isn't dead. I know that because she was here earlier today."

"You saw her?" the sheriff asked.

"After we got back from the hospital, the front door was standing open—Hoyt began to search the house. I smelled her perfume the moment I stepped inside the house."

"Emma," Hoyt pleaded again.

"I smelled her perfume another time when she went through our things in our bedroom. Don't you see what is happening here?" Emma cried. "Aggie is trying to frame my husband. She is so determined to be right."

The sheriff looked uncomfortable.

"Emma, the sheriff isn't here about Aggie Wells," Hoyt said. "This is about Krystal."

Sheriff Crawford nodded solemnly and then Emma knew even before the woman reached into her pocket that there was more. They had found some kind of evidence at the scene.

"I need to ask you, Mr. Chisholm, if this is yours." Sheriff Crawford pushed a small plastic bag across the table. Emma caught sight of something discolored inside it. She recognized it at once—and so did Hoyt.

"Where did you get that?" Emma demanded.

"It was found with Krystal Chisholm's remains."

"That's not possible. Hoyt has his upstairs in his—" Emma was on her feet. She hurried up the stairs and opened the top drawer of Hoyt's bureau and rummaged through the wooden box. She knew she'd seen the bolo tie with the three C's on it in the box. It had to be there.

She found matching cufflinks but no bolo tie. She stood, trying to catch her breath from her panic, her fear, the run up the stairs. She'd been so sure the bolo tie had been in there even though she hadn't seen Hoyt ever wear it.

Returning downstairs, she found the sheriff and her husband waiting for her. Hoyt had his head down, looking like a guilty man. She wanted to snap at him, tell him to knock it off. She knew he was innocent. She knew that the reason he was behaving this way was that he felt responsible because he'd married Krystal, because he thought Aggie Wells had won, as if he'd always feared it was just a matter of time before he was arrested.

Three dead wives. Who wouldn't think he did it?

The sheriff didn't have to ask if Emma had found the bolo tie, but Emma still shook her head, her gaze going to her husband as she slid into the chair next to him and took his hand again.

"Mr. Chisholm?" The sheriff was looking at Hoyt. "Is this yours?"

He nodded, then glanced at the tape recorder she had turned on when the questioning began and said, "Yes, it's mine."

"When was the last time you saw it?" she asked.

He glanced at Emma, then shook his head. "It was part of a bolo tie I haven't worn in years."

"So you weren't aware it was missing?"

"No."

The sheriff rose to her feet. "Hoyt Chisholm? You are under arrest for the murder of Krystal Blake Chisholm."

Emma listened as the sheriff stated her husband his rights. "He didn't kill her," she cried as the sheriff pulled out her handcuffs. Hoyt pushed himself up from the table as if carrying the weight of the world on his broad shoulders. "I'm telling you he couldn't kill *anyone.*"

Her husband turned, gave her a sad smile. "It's going to be all right."

The sheriff gave her a sympathetic look as she led Hoyt out the door. "You might want to call a lawyer for your husband."

Emma could only nod as she watched the sheriff escort Hoyt out to the patrol car, put him in the rear seat and drive away. She knew she should rush to the phone and call his lawyer and his sons, but what she really needed to do was find Aggie Wells.

Or maybe, she thought with a sudden chill as she looked out across the wide open country that was Chisholm Cattle Company, maybe Aggie was planning on finding her.

Chapter Eleven

Billie Rae drove the car down the impossibly narrow road cut into the side of the mountain wondering if she'd lost her mind. She had to creep along, dodging the rocks that would take out the oil pan, while at the same time avoiding the solid rock face of the side of the mountain—and the sheer drop off into the river gorge.

Once she'd turned onto the road, she'd also realized she couldn't change her mind. She would have to go to the end of the road. No way could she back up. She was committed.

"You should be *committed*—to the nut house," she said to herself. More and more she was realizing this was a suicide mission. Desperate times called for— "Just drive."

She could hear the wind rushing down through the gorge. It whistled through the gap in her car window and whipped at what little vegetation grew between the boulders on the mountainside next to her. Ahead she could see the bridge and felt physically ill at the sight of it swaying wildly in the gale.

Billie Rae concentrated on the road and tried not to look—or think—too far ahead. There was literally no turning back now. Duane would be coming soon. She had to get ready. If he caught her now…

Ahead she saw where the road abruptly ended in a pile of rock and dirt. There was just enough room to park the car. She didn't try to turn it around. If her plan worked, she would worry about getting out of here then. It was such a long shot that she would be leaving here at all she wasn't about to take the time now to turn the car around.

Climbing out, she felt the full force of the wind as it roared through the canyon. For a moment she froze as she watched the foot-bridge swing back and forth high above the rocks and dark green water below. Could she do this? Or had she played right into Duane's hands and given him the perfect place to kill her? This would give him such an easy out.

He could get away with her murder if things went wrong and never serve a day in jail for it.

But then, Billie Rae thought no matter where she met him, he would figure out a way to get away with what he planned to do to her anyway. He'd gotten away with murder before. All the odds had been stacked in his favor, they always were. But she promised herself that she would end it here. One way or another.

She glanced at her watch. She could feel time slipping through her fingers. She had to move. *Now!* If Duane caught her just standing here, everything he'd said about her would be true. And everyone knew what happened to cowards.

Billie Rae cautiously moved to the rear of the car, feeling as if she was hanging on the side of the mountain by the skin of her teeth. Opening the trunk, she pulled out the large jacket she'd purchased, then taking the knife, began to cut into the cloth.

This morning after Tanner's call she'd known she had to use her husband's Achilles heel if she hoped to still be alive by dark.

She'd found out about Duane's weakness by accident—something Duane had never forgotten—or forgiven.

"Did you hear about your big, tough husband?" one of the other cops she'd only just met, had asked her after too many drinks. They had been at one of the few parties with his fellow boys in blue that Duane had allowed her to attend—and the last after that night.

"Shut up," Duane said under his breath, but either the cop didn't hear or ignored the warning.

"So here we are chasing a robbery suspect and he hightails it up a six-story fire escape," the cop continues. "Duane starts up after him, me behind him. Then all of a sudden Duane looks down and stops dead. I crash into him and say, 'What the hell?' The dumb bastard, it turns out, is scared of heights." The cop broke up in loud guffaws.

The cop hadn't been watching Duane, but Billie Rae had. His face had been flushed with anger, a vein throbbing in his neck, his hands fisted at his sides. She'd known Duane would never forgive the cop for telling that story—especially in front of her.

Two months later the cop was found shot to death in an alley. No suspect was ever found, but Billie Rae knew who'd killed him—and why. She also knew that had she told the police, no one would have believed her.

Just as no one had believed her the one time she'd tried to report the abuse.

"I'm going to give you some good advice," her husband's captain had told her after she'd taken a taxi down to the police station on a day she knew Duane would be on assignment away from the department. "Go home. Stop fighting with your husband. Work a little harder to make him happy."

Now she glanced again at the bridge hanging suspended over the gorge. She was about to take on the fight of her life with her cop husband. And how it ended would all depend on how badly he wanted to get his hands on her.

TANNER CAME TO in the dark. He was immediately aware of the pain—and his surroundings. He was in the trunk of a fast-moving car.

He could hear the whine of the tires on the highway and smell exhaust. His hands were bound in front of him and he felt cramped even in the roomy space of what he knew was the Lincoln's trunk.

He wiped something sticky and wet from his left eye and tried to sit up. His brother Marshall had been right. He had gone for Duane's throat, charging him after the ambush even though the cop had quickly pulled a gun from under his shirt.

Tanner had gotten in a few good punches, catching the cop off balance. Duane had thought the pistol he pointed at Tanner would deter him. It hadn't. Tanner hadn't thought Duane would shoot him in the casino parking lot but the furious cop had definitely *wanted* to pull the trigger.

Duane had gotten the final blow, though. Tanner hadn't seen the butt of the gun coming until it was too late. He tried to block the blow, but his head had taken the brunt of it.

That's all he remembered although he was sure Duane had kicked him a few times when he was down. His ribs hurt like hell and he felt as if he'd been used for a punching bag.

From what he could tell, there was a cut over his left eye which was bleeding and his nose might be broken.

He had no idea how long he'd been out—or how far they had driven. All he remembered was Duane saying that Billie Rae was waiting for them up the road.

It was too dark to see if there was a latch, something that could get him out of the trunk when the time came. He felt around, trying not to move too much, but didn't find anything. He didn't want the cop to know he was awake. Not yet, anyway.

Tanner felt he had the best chance of survival by pretending to still be knocked out. The element of surprise might be his *only* chance, he thought, remembering the fury in the cop's face when he'd jumped him.

What confused Tanner was how Duane had known he would be at the casino. Billie Rae wouldn't have told him. Tanner swore as he realized how stupid he'd been. Duane was a cop. He probably put a tracking device on Tanner's pickup.

He tried to think of when Duane might have had access to the truck. When Tanner had gone to the hospital to see his brother? The bastard had probably been just waiting for him to lead him to Billie Rae.

BILLIE RAE PUT ON the harness she'd purchased at the climbing store. She attached the rope the way the clerk had shown her, her fingers hardly shaking.

Don't think about all the things that can go wrong.

Don't think about Duane. Or the bridge. Or...Tanner.

Instead, she concentrated on what she had to do as she put the large jacket on over the climbing harness, coiled the rope she'd attached to the harness and put it in one large pocket of the jacket. The gun she put in the other pocket along with the extra cartridges. Hesitating, she took the gun from her pocket, lifted it to chest high and aimed it toward the bridge.

The weight of the weapon in her hands made her feel stronger than she really was, braver, almost invincible. She wondered if that was how Duane felt when he was armed. He spent hours cleaning his gun, handling it, holding it, aiming it. She shuddered at how often he had aimed it at her heart and threatened to blow a hole in her the size of a half dollar.

"You should learn to shoot," Duane said one night after a few beers.

"I don't like guns."

He'd laughed at that. "Only fools don't like guns. A gun can save your life."

"Or take it," she'd said.

He'd smiled at that. "I wouldn't waste a bullet on you, sweetheart. I'd kill you with my bare hands if you ever gave me reason."

The next afternoon, he'd come home early. "Come on," he'd said.

"Where are we going?" It wasn't like him to come home early. She feared something had happened at work and that they would be moving again. She'd only recently learned by overhearing Duane on the phone that something he did in Oklahoma was why he'd applied to the force in Williston, North Dakota. He'd told her it was because the job paid more but she'd found out that too had been a lie.

She'd later learned that he'd assaulted one of the suspects who'd said something to him that set him off. Two other policemen had been forced to pull him off the suspect. Unfortunately for Duane, some witness had gotten a little of it on his cell phone camera.

His fellow cops had covered for him so Duane had managed to get off with little more than a slap on the wrist, but the department was watching him—something Duane couldn't handle.

"We're going to the shooting range," he had announced the day he'd come home early. "No wife of mine is going to be afraid of guns."

"I'm not afraid, I just don't—"

"You're going to learn to shoot—and shoot well." She'd heard the warning in his tone and knew there was no arguing with Duane once he'd made up his mind.

Now she quickly slipped the gun into her jacket pocket again. Learning to shoot had been the one thing Duane had taught her that was finally going to come in handy.

The wind blew her hair into her eyes. She tied it back but still some tendrils escaped. Then she doubled-checked to make sure she had everything, before she glanced at her watch again. Duane could be here any minute.

Slamming the trunk, she turned to look again at the bridge.

It was made of wooden slats that were no more than four feet wide. They were bound together with what appeared to be rope. Two other ropes that stretched from bank to bank acted as handrails. Each of those was attached vertically to the bridge platform every four or five feet with more rope.

Two steel cables anchored in concrete on each side ran under the bridge to give it reinforced support. But the cables were slack enough to let the bridge move and, boy, was it moving.

From this angle, it swayed in the wind as hypnotically as a pendulum. Billie Rae couldn't imagine trying to walk out on it—or how she would get to the middle where she needed to be when Duane arrived. She just knew she had to take that first step—just as she'd taken the first step to be free of Duane.

This time, she let herself think of Tanner as she slipped down the steep rocky slope to the bridge entrance. She was terrified of what she was about to do. Thinking of Tanner

Chisholm gave her strength. At the base of the footbridge, she had to climb up to get on it.

A chain had been stretched across the opening with another sign that warned that the bridge was for authorized personnel only. Violators would be prosecuted. Like so many signs she'd seen out west, this sign had been used for target practice. It was peppered with rusted gunshot holes.

The holes made it hard—but not impossible—to read the smaller print at the bottom of the sign: Danger: Do Not Cross In High Wind.

She watched the wind kick up dust from the other side of the mountain, a gust wildly rocking the bridge before it settled back into just swinging.

Gathering all her courage, Billie Rae ducked under the sign and crawled up onto the bridge.

JUST THE THOUGHT OF Aggie Wells pulling their strings as if they were puppets made Emma angry. She had to calm down before she went back into the house after the sheriff left with Hoyt. She called the lawyer first, then each of her stepsons.

"Dad didn't kill anyone," said Dawson, the eldest of the brothers and the one they all agreed was the most responsible of the six. "Don't worry. We can take care of the ranch until we get him out. Have you called his lawyer?"

"Yes, he's headed down to the sheriff's department to see about getting Hoyt out on bail," Emma told him—just as she had the others.

That wasn't the problem—getting Hoyt out on bail, she thought after she hung up. It was finding Aggie Wells and getting at the truth. No way did Emma believe it was a coincidence that Aggie's car ended up abandoned near where Krystal's body was found. Or that the bolo tie clasp had ended up at the site.

Unless Hoyt is guilty.

The thought flew at her out of the darkness of her thoughts.

"My husband is not a killer," she said to the empty kitchen. Her voice echoed back at her and, with a chill, she realized how alone she was. The cook, Celeste, had called and made a lame excuse for why she couldn't make it today. Housekeeper Mae had called shortly after with an equally weak excuse. They were bailing off Chisholm Cattle Company as if it were a sinking ship.

She couldn't really blame them. Nor could she bear to think of Hoyt locked up—let alone him going to prison for a murder, or murders he didn't commit. Aggie Wells had to be behind this.

And if that was the case…Emma let out a cry as a thought struck her. *Aggie killed Krystal. How else would she know where the woman was buried so she could implicate Hoyt by putting the silver bolo tie clasp at the scene?*

She started to reach for the phone to call the sheriff when she realized she had no proof. It was all conjecture. She couldn't prove the bolo tie had been in Hoyt's jewelry box and he didn't seem to remember if it had been there or not since he'd said he hadn't worn it in years.

"Hoyt didn't do it." She said it loud enough that if the house wanted to argue she was up for it. All she got was an echo and realized she was arguing with herself because she was scared.

She was convinced Aggie Wells was alive and behind this. But did she really believe the former insurance investigator had gone so far off the rails that she would murder Hoyt's third wife just to frame him? That did seem extreme.

But Aggie had already been investigating the deaths of Hoyt's first two wives. What if she'd become so frustrated for lack of proof that she'd decided to kill Krystal and make it look as if Hoyt had, just so she could frame him?

"And then wait almost thirty years before she made sure the woman's remains were found?" Emma demanded of the empty room.

She was glad she hadn't called the sheriff. Her theory sounded way too far-fetched.

Just the fact that she'd smelled the woman's perfume in the house twice hardly proved that Aggie Wells was alive. Which begged the question, why hadn't she turned up?

Emma poured herself a mug of coffee and cut a small piece of the oatmeal cake. After staring down at the small piece of a cake for a long moment, she cut herself a larger piece as a thought crossed her mind.

If she really believed in Hoyt's innocence—which she did—then she needed to figure out what Aggie had been doing in her house. She took a bite of the cake. She really did make the best oatmeal cake, she thought, as she swallowed and had a sip of coffee. She could feel her strength coming back as well as her senses.

The reason for Aggie coming to the house at least the first time came to her like a shot out of the dark.

Aggie took Hoyt's bolo tie to frame him.

Emma felt a chill as she realized that had to be it. All of their bureau drawers had been gone through including Emma's jewelry box. She hadn't thought to check Hoyt's because he'd glanced in and said he didn't think anything was missing.

The only clue had been that lingering scent the woman had left behind. Emma had recognized it when she'd met Aggie at the bar at Sleeping Buffalo. When she'd accused Aggie of snooping around their ranch house, Aggie hadn't denied it. She'd given Emma the impression that she had merely been curious—and concerned—about Emma, Hoyt's fourth wife, after what had apparently happened to the other three.

Sitting up straighter, Emma saw how foolish she had been not to see this before. Aggie was so determined to prove Hoyt had murdered his first wife that she had become obsessed with being right. It had apparently cost Aggie her job at the insurance company.

But if she had killed Krystal... Emma had a thought that felt so right it scared her. What if Aggie hadn't killed Krystal to frame Hoyt—but to get rid of the competition?

Hoyt was an incredibly handsome man—not to mention wealthy and respected, a great catch. If Aggie had fallen for him while investigating him...

It fit. She wished she could ask Hoyt how Aggie had acted after his third wife had disappeared. Of course Aggie would have investigated the disappearance. That meant she'd been in Whitehorse, probably had been out to the ranch to talk to Hoyt.

But Hoyt hadn't been interested. He'd sworn

off women all those years until he'd met Emma—and Aggie Wells had come back into his life. How would a jealous woman react to Hoyt getting married again after all those years?

Badly, Emma thought. So badly, though, that she would make sure Krystal's body turned up and that her own didn't? So obsessed that she had faked her own disappearance and made it look as if she too had been murdered?

Emma hugged herself as she realized just how obsessed that was. If she was right, then Aggie Wells was a very dangerous person with a very jealous streak.

She glanced toward the window, uneasy at the direction her thoughts had taken. The day was bright and sunny, the sky a brilliant blue, not a cloud in sight. Still she felt a chill wrap itself around her neck like a noose. Where was Aggie right now? Was she hiding in the hills, watching the house with binoculars? That seemed unlikely.

If Aggie wasn't hiding in the hills watching the house with a pair of binoculars then how had she known earlier that there was no one around so she could come back into the house again?

Emma took the last bite of cake and almost choked as the answer came to her.

Aggie Wells had bugged the house!

THE MOMENT BILLIE RAE stepped onto the bridge, she made her first mistake. Still on her hands and knees after slipping under the chain across the bridge entrance, she'd looked down. The rushing movement of the dark green water over the rocks far below threw her off balance.

She closed her eyes, held on to the wooden slats of the bridge beneath her and tried to regain not only her breath—but her courage.

After a few moments, she opened her eyes, this time focusing on the other side of the gorge as she got to her feet. This end of the bridge was attached to a concrete base set back into the side of the mountain so the bridge was fairly stable.

But the moment she took her first step, she felt the bridge move under her weight. She clutched the ropes that formed the handrail. They felt insubstantial. She didn't look through the gaping hole on each side between the rope or through the wooden slats of the bridge beneath her feet, but she was well aware of how easily it would be to fall between the bridge floor and the handrail rope uprights and drop the fifty feet to the river and rocks below.

She couldn't move for a moment. The wind blowing down the canyon buffeted her hair, sending tendrils into her eyes. She could hear the river and the wind and a semi shifting down on the highway off in the distance, but she couldn't take a step—just as she hadn't all those years ago.

She'd been eleven the first time she'd ever seen a bridge like this. A boy she'd liked had asked her to go on a picnic with his family. The bridge spanned across a creek only about fifteen feet above the water. Nor was the bridge very long.

The boy had scampered across it and turned to look back at her, daring her to cross. She hadn't liked the feel of it, the way the footbridge swayed with each step she took, or the way the boy was watching her intently.

She'd gotten halfway across when the boy had started making it rock violently. Instinctively, she'd dropped to her hands and knees and gripped the rough edges of the worn boards in her hands and couldn't move.

The boy had felt badly for scaring her, for making her cry. He'd stopped rocking the bridge and offered to help her up, but she'd wanted nothing to do with him or his help and ordered him to leave her alone.

His father had come and talked her off the bridge. She'd never forgotten being in the middle of that bridge on her hands and knees. She'd never felt so trapped and nakedly vulnerable—until she found herself married to an abusive cop who would rather see her dead than free her.

At the sound of a car engine, Billie Rae turned her head to look back toward the road down to the bridge. Duane's large black car came to a stop on the rim of the gorge.

She turned back to the bridge and with an urgency born of survival, she took a step, then another, desperately needing to reach the swaying middle before Duane came after her.

BUGGED? EMMA ALMOST LAUGHED at how ridiculous she sounded and yet she went straight to the computer and typed in: How to tell if a house is bugged?

To her amazement a list came up with not only inexpensive listening devices that could be purchased by anyone, but video surveillance devices as well. She'd had no idea how small or how high-tech the devices had become.

Just the thought that Aggie Wells could have been not only listening to their every word—but also watching them all this time—gave her more than a chill. As she read what to do about the problem, she realized that if Aggie was watching, Emma didn't want her to know that she was on to her.

Under the pretense of cleaning, she began to search the house for what the article called "conspicuous" places bugs or small video cameras could be hidden: lamps, picture frames, books, under tables and chairs, inside pots and vases. She hoped the sound of the vacuum would mask what she was up to—even if Aggie was watching her.

The devices were made to look like something else or hide in a plant or the edge of a frame on the wall, she'd read. Aggie could be watching her clean right now on a remote device as ordinary as a computer screen or even a cell phone. So Emma knew she had to be very careful if she didn't want to give herself away.

She discovered the first bug quite by accident. She was vacuuming the rug next to the bed when she noticed tiny pieces of plaster. It wasn't the first time she'd seen them in the same spot. The last time she'd been too distracted to think much about it since the house was old and the plastered ceiling had small cracks where the house had shifted.

But now she froze and slowly looked up to the smoke alarm on the ceiling. Her heart began to pound. The smoke alarm was new. Why hadn't she noticed it before? It was small and round and nothing like the other smoke alarms in the house.

Emma knew she'd been staring at it for weeks since some nights she couldn't sleep and— With a shudder, she realized Aggie had been listening to everything Emma and Hoyt had said in this bedroom. In this bed.

Furious, she wanted to take the vacuum attachment and beat the device off the ceiling.

She had to refrain from doing that, though, if she hoped to find Aggie. Somehow she had to use this in her favor.

Leaving the vacuum running, she dragged a chair over and climbed up on it to inspect the smoke alarm. It didn't appear to have video. That was a relief.

Taking the advice she'd picked up on the internet, she put on headphones, then using her radio dial, listened near the smoke alarm for uniform distortion. The bleeps and recurring patterns indicated the presence of a covert listening device—just as the directions had said.

She finished vacuuming up the flakes of plaster that installing the alarm had caused. Not just installing it, Emma thought. Aggie had come back to the house a second time and messed with the alarm. Had it not been working properly? She could only hope.

Moving through the rest of the house, this time Emma knew what to look for and quickly found three more new smoke alarms. She could understand now why none of the family had noticed them. The devices were small and unobtrusive. The one in the kitchen was hidden on the other side of the overhead light, same with the ones in the dining room and living room.

Emma put the vacuum away, went back into the kitchen and poured herself a cup of coffee before sitting down at the table to plot the best way to draw Aggie Wells out into the open.

She had a feeling it wouldn't be necessary if Aggie thought she was alone at the house. Emma remembered how Aggie had repeatedly warned her that she would be the next wife of Hoyt Chisholm's to die.

She curled her fingers around the warmth of the mug. If Aggie had just been waiting for the time when Emma would be all alone in his big rambling ranch house, this was the time. No Hoyt. No stepsons. No cook or housekeeper. Just Emma, the fourth wife of Hoyt Chisholm.

Chapter Twelve

Duane could not believe what he was seeing. He'd turned off where Billie Rae had told him to, driven down the narrow dirt road, but when he'd come to where the road disappeared over the edge into the gorge, he'd thrown on his brakes with a curse thinking she'd meant to kill him.

Now as he stood next to the car, listening to the wind whistling down the river canyon, he hoped to hell he *was* seeing things. Billie Rae didn't really expect him to drive down that road cut into the side of the mountain, did she?

"What the hell were you thinking, woman?" he yelled. The wind blew his words back at him.

That's when he spotted her. She was standing at the entrance to a foot bridge that hung high above the river gorge. Who *was* this woman? Not the woman he'd married. Billie Rae had never been daring. He scoffed at even the idea. If anything he would have said his wife was timid. He thought of the way she often cowered away from him, which only made him more angry with her at the time.

So what had happened to her?

He frowned as he took in the small red compact car she apparently had been driving. Where the hell had she gotten that? From that cowboy? Or some other man she'd told her hard-luck story to? He ground his teeth at the thought that she'd told people about him. What went on between them was private. She had no business sharing anything personal with another person.

He watched Billie Rae start across the bridge.

"What are you doing?" he yelled again. She didn't seem to hear him as she took another step, then another.

He looked from her to the road. No way was he driving his car any farther down this road. He reached back inside the Lincoln, pulled on his shoulder holster and, on impulse grabbed the small unregistered handgun he'd taken off a drug dealer in Oklahoma. He stuffed it into the waistband of his slacks, covered it with his shirt, and slammed the car door.

As he walked away, he hit the automatic lock on his keys, heard it beep once, then pocketed his keys.

Billie Rae had stopped on the bridge. She was clinging to the rope rails. What was she doing out there in the first place? The damned fool woman must have changed her mind knowing he was going to be furious with her and now she was trying to get away from him by crossing the river?

He glanced to the other side and saw only a narrow trail that led to what appeared to be some kind of weather station box used by meteorologists. The trail ended abruptly. Billie Rae was only going to find herself at another dead end. The stupid damned woman.

Well, if she thought he was going out on that bridge after her, she was sadly mistaken. She could just figure out how to get back and when she did, he would be waiting for her.

The road was rocky and rough and the dress shoes he was wearing were all wrong for chasing his wife into a river gorge. Duane swore as he started down the road, telling himself he would make Billie Rae rue this day.

TANNER HAD FELT THE BIG CAR slow, then turn onto a bumpy road. Is this where the cop was meeting Billie Rae? Or was this where he was getting rid of the passenger in the trunk?

He'd listened. Earlier he'd heard stereo music and even at one point, Duane signing along. The man couldn't carry a tune.

Tanner had tried hard not to bounce around on the rough road. He was hoping that Duane, in his hurry to get to Billie Rae, had forgotten about him. At least he was driving slow now—no doubt to protect his car—not his passenger.

The Lincoln had finally come to a sudden stop, throwing Tanner hard against the trunk wall. He had lain dazed, blinking in the darkness as he heard Duane get out of the car.

He heard the wind and then the cop swear. Tanner thought he smelled the river. Or at least water. All his senses seemed more acute.

He felt something against his hip and realized it was his cell phone. It had fallen out of his pocket. He hadn't even thought to check for it, just assuming Duane would have taken it.

Picking it up, he hit 911. When the operator came on, he whispered, "Someone is about to be murdered. I don't know where I am. I'm locked in the trunk of a black Lincoln with North Dakota plates, off the road, north of Great Falls. Hurry."

He disconnected as he heard Duane get back into the car and cut the engine. This must be where Billie Rae had told Duane to meet her. Was she outside the car? He listened but didn't hear her voice, but he'd heard Duane yelling earlier though he hadn't been able to make out what he'd been saying with the howling wind rocking the car.

Tanner felt an overwhelming need to call her, let her know the police were on their way, but he'd feared with the music and motor shut off, the cop would be able to hear him since he could hear the cop moving around in the front seat. The car shifted as Duane got out again, slamming the door.

Tanner held his breath, assuming Duane

would be walking back to the trunk and that any moment the lid would swing open and—

He heard a beep and the doors all lock. Then there was nothing but the sound of the wind outside the car.

Listening hard, Tanner tried now to gauge how much time had passed. He keyed in the number of his old cell phone and prayed Billie Rae would answer.

BILLIE RAE WASN'T SURE she could do this. She'd never been afraid of heights, but as she started across the swaying bridge, she felt motion sickness roil in her stomach.

She took another step, sliding her hand along the rope railing to where it connected with the lower part of the bridge, forcing herself to let go and reach for another section of rope. The bridge swayed beneath her like a writhing snake.

Don't look down.

She thought she'd heard Duane yelling something at her, but realized she may have only imagined his angry bellow.

Then she heard him. Duane was yelling at her, his voice closer. She couldn't look back.

She wasn't even sure now if she could pull off her plan because it meant not only reaching the middle of the bridge, but also turning around.

She kept moving, one step, then another. The wind whipped her hair around her face, rocked the bridge and kicked up dust from the mountain on each side of the gorge. She didn't look back, couldn't. Just a little farther.

She stumbled on one of the boards that had bowed in the weather and almost fell. Tightening her grip on the rope on each side of her, she froze as she tried to catch her breath. Her heart was pounding so hard it hurt.

As she started to take another step, her cell phone rang. She'd stuck the phone in the pocket of her slacks earlier and had forgotten about it. The phone rang again.

She stopped moving across the bridge, willing herself not to look down. Gripping the ropes on each side of the narrow footbridge, she turned her head just enough that she could see the road cut into the side of the mountain. Duane was half way down the road, coming on foot. She squinted at the bright sun, the wind in her hair and the bridge swaying under her feet.

She'd thought it would be Duane calling her. But he wasn't on his cell phone. That meant... Tanner was calling. A bubble rose in her chest. He would have reached the casino by now and be waiting for her. The phone rang again.

Billie Rae thought of him worrying about her. She knew it was foolish, what she was about to do. She needed to get to the middle of the bridge. Duane was coming. The man was crazy. Who knew what he would do?

But she also desperately needed to hear Tanner's voice right now. She was too aware that it was probably going to be the last time she heard it.

Letting go of one of the rope railings, she started to reach into her pocket. The bridge rocked wildly in a gust of wind and she lost her balance. She grabbed for the rope railing again, her fingers closing on it. Her heart lodged in her throat so tightly she could hardly draw a breath.

The phone rang again and she let out a cry of frustration and pain. She steadied herself, praying that Tanner wouldn't hang up before she could get the phone out of her pocket. She dug it out, balancing her weight on the bridge and trying hard not to think about Duane coming up the road toward her.

"Hello?" She had to raise her voice over the wind.

"Billie Rae, where are you?"

She couldn't speak; his voice filled her with sudden warmth and made her ache for what could have been.

"I called the police. They'll be here soon."

She felt her pulse begin to race. *"Here?"*

"I'm in the trunk of Duane's car. Tell me if he's far enough away that I can try to bust out."

She looked back toward Duane's car. "No," she said into the phone. "You shouldn't be here. Please don't—" The bridge rocked in another gust of wind, throwing her off balance again. She dropped the phone. It hit at her feet, bounced once, then fell between the bridge slats.

She watched the cell phone drop to the deep green of the river and rocks far below as she grabbed wildly at the rope, missing it, then lurching for it again. Her fingers clamped over the line and she teetered between the two ropes, her pulse thundering in her ears as she fought to regain her balance again.

"What the hell are you doing?" Duane's angry bellow sounded as if he was right behind her. He must have run the last stretch and was now at the other end of the bridge.

She didn't dare look back for fear he would be racing along the bridge toward her. Concentrating on nothing but her next step, she slid her hands along the weathered ropes, letting go only to grab the next section.

"Billie Rae, you stupid bitch! Get back here now!" Out of the corner of her eyes, she caught glimpses of deep green through the gaps between the wooden slats of the bridge floor as she took a step—just enough to remind her what was at stake if she failed.

"If I have to come after you…"

She heard a creak, felt the rope railing on her right grow taut and knew without looking that Duane was on the bridge behind her.

TANNER FELT AN URGENCY like none he'd ever experienced before. Something in Billie

Rae's voice. Where was she? Close by. He'd heard the sound of the wind and a creak of boards. But it was what he'd heard beneath her words that had him frantically shifting his body around so his feet were pointed at the back seat of the Lincoln.

He prayed that Duane was far enough from the car that he wouldn't hear the noise and come back, but he couldn't wait any longer.

He kicked the back seat, putting as much force as he could into it given how cramped his surroundings were. He kicked harder. He felt the seat give a little.

Repositioning himself, he braced against the wall of the trunk and kicked and pushed as hard as he could. He felt the seat give a little more.

He stopped to listen, afraid he would hear the beep of Duane unlocking the car doors—or worse, the trunk lid.

Hearing nothing but the wind, Tanner kicked again and again. The seat finally gave. He lay in the trunk breathing hard, then gave the seat a final push. He could see light coming in through the rear tinted windows.

Just a little more....

As HE STEPPED OUT ONTO the bridge, Duane watched the water far below and felt the muscles in his legs begin to spasm. It was all he could do to keep standing. He clung to the rope rail, feeling sick to his stomach.

He couldn't move, couldn't breathe. Acrophobia. That's what the doctor had called it.

"It's not unusual," the mandatory police department psychiatrist had told him after the fire escape incident. "A large percentage of the population has the same problem."

"Acrophobia? What the hell is that?"

"It's an extreme or irrational fear of heights."

"Are you saying I'm irrational?" he'd demanded.

"It means that sufferers of acrophobia experience panic attacks in high places and often become too agitated to get themselves down. Isn't that what happened to you, Officer?"

Duane raised his gaze to look down the swaying footbridge to where Billie Rae had stopped moving. Maybe she was coming back. At the thought, he felt a rush of relief, of gratitude, almost love. If she came back, he wouldn't be forced to go out any farther on this bridge.

Maybe he wouldn't kill her. He'd just make her wish she was dead.

"I'm glad to see you've come to your senses," he called to her. "If you'd made me come after you…"

You don't want me to have to come after you.

Duane was startled by the sound of his old man's voice echoing in his head.

So what's it going to be, sonny? You think you can get away from me? You want to try? Or are you going to take what's coming to you like a man?

He'd been six years old that day when he'd stood in the field, his father standing at the edge of the barn door with a thick leather strap dangling from one large hand.

You going to take your medicine like a man or am I going to have to come after you? I guess I don't have to tell you what's going to happen if I have to come after you, do I, Duane?

"Come on back now, Billie Rae," he called to her when she still hadn't moved. He could tell by the way she was balanced on the bridge, her head and shoulders slumped, that she'd scared herself. She didn't want to go any farther. She would come back now.

"You want me, Duane?" she called back over one shoulder. "Then you're going to have to come get me. I can't move."

He swore under his breath. Hell, he'd just leave her there. She'd either starve or lose her balance and fall. Either way would work for him.

But his need to teach her a lesson with his hands pulled at him, taunting him. "Damn it, Billie Rae."

Duane looked back over his shoulder. It wasn't that far back to solid ground. If he turned around now… He started to, but then he saw Billie Rae glance back at him and remembered the night that dumb cop had told her he was afraid of heights. It was bad enough that she'd left him, bad enough that she'd put him through all of this, but now she was almost daring him to come out on the bridge.

Unless you're too afraid, you coward.

He stared at her, realizing she didn't think

he could do it. She was planning on him getting scared and...what? Falling?

"You've made a big mistake," he called to her as he took a step toward her, then another. "You think I won't come get you?" His laugh echoed on the wind. "Oh, I'll come get you, Billie Rae. But you are going to wish to hell and gone that you hadn't done this."

SQUIRMING AROUND, TANNER worked his torso through the opening he'd made by kicking the back seat free. Now he just needed something to cut the plastic handcuffs. He managed to get the rear door open and dropped to his feet outside the car.

With a shock, he took in his surroundings. Duane had parked the car only feet from the edge of a precipice. Tanner stared at the river gorge for a moment wondering where the cop had gone. Was he really meeting Billie Rae here?

His stomach knotted at the thought.

He quickly reached into the car and unlatched the trunk. In the back, he found what he was looking for. A pair of pliers. He worked the pliers between his wrists, snapped the handles shut and snipped the plastic. The cuffs fell away.

For a few seconds, he searched through the tools to see if there was anything he could use as a weapon. He chose the tire iron, saw that it had what looked like dried blood on it, and quietly closed the trunk.

As he neared the rim of the river gorge, he peered over, saw the deep gorge, then looked upriver to where the narrow road that had been cut in the side of the mountain ended at a footbridge.

His heart dropping, he saw Billie Rae had stopped part way across the footbridge—the cop close behind.

Tanner began to run, the wind and dust blowing in his face, fear gripping him. He didn't want to think of what was going to happen when Duane caught up with her on the bridge.

Tanner wouldn't be able to reach Duane before he got to Billie Rae. The treacherous road made running at any speed almost impossible. Duane was now slowly moving across the bridge going after Billie Rae.

He could hear Duane yelling. So far, the

cop hadn't seen him. Tanner had a feeling that Duane had forgotten about him. The wind howled in his ears. He could smell the river and the dust that kicked up along the steep bank of the gorge.

Billie Rae had started to move again, but the cop seemed to be gaining on her. Tanner ran up behind the car she'd bought. The cop still hadn't seen him apparently. He noticed that Duane was wearing a shoulder holster but he hadn't reached for his gun. Instead, he was holding onto both ropes suspended across the river gorge as if his life depended on it as he continued across the bridge after Billie Rae.

Tanner ran from behind the car over to the entrance of the bridge. A gust of wind whirled up dust around him and rocked the bridge wildly.

Billie Rae had reached the middle of the bridge. Suddenly she seemed to lose her balance. He felt panic seize his chest as he saw her drop to her hands and knees on the footbridge.

Duane was yelling obscenities at her as he clutched at the rope railing, the bridge swinging crazily. The cop was staring down at the river and rocks far below him. He wasn't looking at Billie Rae.

But Tanner was.

He saw her reach into the pocket of the large jacket she wore and attach what looked like a length of climbing rope to the steel cable that held the suspended footbridge in place.

Then she got to her feet again and turned around so she was facing Duane who was still yards away, the rope hidden behind her leg.

Tanner watched her hand sink into the pocket of the jacket again. He let out a silent groan, then said under his breath, "What are you doing, Billie Rae?" as he crawled up and onto the bridge behind Duane.

BILLIE RAE LOOKED DOWN the stretch of bridge swaying in the wind, estimating how many feet lay between her and Duane. He had stopped and now stood as if petrified and unable to move.

Unfortunately he hadn't come far enough out onto the bridge. She needed him to come at least another ten feet toward her—and the middle of the bridge.

Even from here she could see that his face was flushed, the large vessel in his neck bulging with fury and no doubt fear. It was a wonder he didn't give himself a heart attack, she thought.

"Get your ass back here, Billie Rae," he yelled, but his bellow had lost a lot of its bravado.

He didn't want to come out on the bridge. He was scared.

She saw how easily her plan could fail if he suddenly turned tail and rushed back toward the safety of the mountainside.

Worse, she realized with a start, Tanner had gotten out of the trunk of the Lincoln. A moment before he'd been behind her car, but now he had mounted the bridge and was coming up behind Duane.

If Duane turned now, he would see Tanner. She could see that Duane had on his shoulder holster. That meant he'd brought his Glock. She didn't doubt for a moment that he would shoot Tanner in a heartbeat.

"Duane," she called trying to sound as pathetic as he thought she was. She had to get him to come toward her another ten feet—six at the minimum. "I can't move…" Her voice broke. "I'm…scared."

He glared at her as if he thought she was mocking him. He stood with his feet spread apart as he tried to keep his balance, his hands gripping the ropes.

"Please," she cried. "You're going to have to help me."

"If I have to come out there, only one of us will be coming back," Duane yelled.

"You don't mean that."

"The hell I don't. It ends here, Billie Rae. I can't have a wife like you, don't you get it?"

She got it. "And I can't have a husband like you," she said under her breath. "Then just leave me here," she called back. "Divorce me."

He smiled, then let out a laugh. "You'd like that, wouldn't you?" The laugh died on his lips as they twisted into a snarl. "Over *your* dead body."

Her heart pounded as Duane took another step toward her, then another.

Come on, Duane. Just keep coming.

He stumbled on probably the same board she had and almost fell. He grabbed hold of the ropes, clinging to them. His face was livid with fury and fear. She could see the white of his knuckles on the rope and knew he was thinking about wrapping those fingers around her throat.

"We can stop this right now," she called to him. "You realize I'm not going to be your wife any longer—one way or the other."

"You got that right."

"Duane, I'm not going to let you hurt me again."

He laughed. "Then I suggest you jump."

He took another step toward her.

Billie Rae didn't dare look past him to where Tanner was cautiously moving along the bridge as to not let Duane know he was back there. She knew that she couldn't change her mind now. She'd come this far and if she wanted this to end, she knew there was no other way out.

That night after the day she'd stopped by the police station to report the abuse, Duane had almost killed her. She should have known Duane's boss would tell him that she had come down to the police station. She'd realized then that there was no restraining order or locked door that could protect her from the man she'd married.

And that was how they had ended up on this bridge, she thought. It had all come down to this moment.

Duane took another step toward her. She gauged the distance and reached into her other pocket and carefully closed her hand around the grip of the gun.

"It will be extremely effective at from four to seven feet. Seven to ten feet is optimum," the sales clerk had told her.

Billie Rae knew she couldn't let Duane get too close. If he lunged for her—

"It doesn't have to be this way," she called to him. "There is no shame in divorce."

The word shame seemed to strike a nerve. Duane swore and took another step toward her and another. Billie Rae watched him, gauging the distance.

She could see that he was perspiring heavily. He was fighting looking down, gripping the ropes. Each step was costing him dearly.

"The hell you will shame me, you stupid bitch," he spat as he lurched toward her.

Billie Rae felt a tremor inside her. Duane

was closing the distance between them quicker than she'd thought he would—or could.

Had she really believed he would let her go, agree to a divorce, stop this craziness?

He had left her no choice, she told herself as he advanced. As if she'd ever had a choice from the day she'd married him.

Duane lumbered forward, grabbing the rope in his big fists, lurching on the wildly swinging footbridge. His anger had trumped his fear. He was too blind with rage to even realize he was suspended fifty feet over a rocky gorge on nothing more than a few boards beneath his feet.

Now. She had to act now or... Billie Rae told herself she could do this. Only a few more feet and if she didn't do something...

The warning signs had been there. She'd noticed even before they'd married that Duane always had to have his way. When she'd tried to assert herself, they'd argued. He had a temper and said hurtful things, but he was always sorry.

She found giving in to him was easier. She hated fighting with him. She overlooked his moodiness and believed if she tried harder to make him happy, everything would be fine. She loved him. And he loved her.

She shuddered as she saw the pattern their lives had taken, her walking around on eggshells, Duane getting furious over nothing at all. Her trying to pacify him. Him needing to be pacified more and more.

And finally Duane taking out all that anger inside him on her.

Billie Rae suddenly thought of the boy her husband had shot soon after they'd moved to Williston. There'd been an investigation, which had put Duane in one of his moods. She'd tried to stay out of his way, but he'd finally come looking for her as if he'd needed to work off some steam by picking a fight with her and slapping her around.

But she remembered what he'd said about the killing.

"The boy was asking for it, so it was self-defense."

"I thought he didn't have a weapon?" she'd foolishly pointed out.

He'd given her one of his dirty looks and raised his fists. "See these? They're a weapon. So that makes it self-defense. Even if my weapon that day was a lot bigger and a hell of a lot more lethal."

Fifteen feet, twelve, ten.

Billie Rae thought of that boy as she pulled the gun from her jacket pocket and said, "That's far enough, Duane."

Chapter Thirteen

Duane froze in mid-step as he saw her pull a gun from the pocket of the oversized jacket she wore. He'd wondered where she'd gotten the jacket since she'd left home without one, didn't have her purse so shouldn't have had money to buy one and this one was too large for her. The cowboy. She must have gotten it from him.

"What do you think you're doing, Billie Rae?" His voice sounded amused even to him. Then he remembered the day he'd taught Billie Rae to shoot.

At first she'd been afraid of the gun, which really made him angry. Then she'd finally taken it and seemed to draw on some inner strength because when she'd fired the automatic pistol she hadn't stopped firing until she'd completely obliterated the bull's eye of the target.

He'd been astounded. "Are you sure you haven't fired a gun before?" he'd demanded.

"I told you, I don't like guns."

Duane realized now that she hadn't answered his question about whether or not she'd fired a gun before. Clearly she had.

"Billie Rae, I thought you didn't like guns," he called to her.

"I don't," she called back. "But you've really given me no choice, have you, Duane?"

"You can't shoot your own husband. Come on, put the gun away before you shoot yourself."

In the years he'd been a cop, he'd faced his share of fools with weapons. He'd learned the telltale nervous gestures that could signal if the hand holding the gun was going to pull the trigger.

He stared at his wife now as if looking at a stranger. Her expression was one of calm, cold and calculating. Her eyes were on him, the gun aimed at his chest, her feet spread as she balanced on the moving bridge.

"You can't be serious," he said, even though

he knew she was. It went against everything he believed about his wife. Even after that humiliating experience at the gun range, if anyone had asked him if Billie Rae could fire a gun at a human being, he would have guffawed and said the woman didn't have the killer instinct. Now he wasn't so sure.

Could she shoot her own husband?

A few days ago he would have thought the question ridiculous.

Right now, though, he had a bad feeling not only could she, she would.

The only question was whether or not he could draw and shoot her before she got off a shot.

He squinted his eyes against the afternoon sun as he tried to see what kind of gun she held in her hands. "What the hell?" he said when he saw that it was a pistol-shaped taser.

As part of his law enforcement training, he'd been hit with a taser and he'd nailed more than a few suspects with one. He was well aware of what happened when fifty-thousand volts traveling in two small darts struck a body.

His gaze shot to the vertical rope supports

every four to five feet along the footbridge and knew that if she pulled the trigger before he reached one, he was in for a long fall—and certain death in the river and rocks below.

Just as Billie Rae had obviously planned it, he realized with a start. The woman had brought him here to kill him.

"You better hope to hell you miss," Duane screamed and lunged forward.

BILLIE RAE WATCHED IN horror as Duane threw himself forward as if he planned to run down the bridge and take the taser from her.

She pulled the trigger. The fifty-thousand volts shot out in two darts that penetrated his shirt to prick his skin.

Her heart in her throat, she saw him instantly lose all muscle control and drop, just like the clerk who'd sold her the taser said would happen.

Duane landed hard on the bridge and would have fallen over the side except for one of the vertical ropes between the footbridge base and the rope handrails.

She only had an instant to stuff the taser into her pocket again and grab the rope before the bridge swung crazily with his fallen weight. Beyond him, she saw Tanner do the same. He was still yards from Duane.

He had stopped and was looking at her as if he couldn't believe what she'd just done. She couldn't, either. Worse, her plan hadn't worked.

Billie Rae clung to the ropes as a gust of wind rocked the bridge and she realized what Duane had done. He'd seen that she had a taser, he'd known what it would do and he'd managed to get to a spot on the bridge so the rope uprights kept him from falling off and dropping to the river below.

A sob rose in her throat as she watched him lying there. A part of her couldn't believe she'd shot him—even with only a taser. Worse, that her plan had been for him to fall from the bridge.

She closed her eyes against the image of him lying bloody and broken in the rocks below. Even though she knew it was him or her in the end, she felt sick to her stomach. How had it come down to this?

With a jolt she realized that she had only a few minutes before he regained control of his body. He would be even more furious. There was no doubt now that he would kill her, that she had chosen the spot she would die today.

Her gaze went to Tanner. They would both die here today. Another sob rose in her throat. She was about to get them both killed.

"Stay back!" she called to Tanner, but he either didn't hear or refused to heed her warning as he began moving toward the spot where Duane had fallen to the bridge slats. Tanner had something in his hand. Something that gleamed in the sunlight. A tire iron?

Duane began to move. Billie Rae saw him trying to get his Glock out of his shoulder holster. He fumbled the gun out, lost his grip. The gun skittered across the planes of the footbridge to drop over the edge. Duane made a guttural sound, then reached for the gun butt sticking out of the waistband of his slacks.

Billie Rae let go of the rope rail with one hand and dug in her pocket for the taser and another cartridge. The wind seemed stronger now. Her eyes burned from it and balancing on the moving bridge was becoming harder, especially as she hurriedly tried to reload the taser.

With shaking fingers she took out the spent cartridge and fumbled to get the new one loaded into the butt-end of the taser, while out of the corner of her eye she watched Duane rise up, the gun in his hand.

A gust of wind swung the bridge. She dropped the cartridge. Like the cell phone, it hit at her feet, bounced and disappeared over the side of the footbridge.

Billie Rae let out a cry of frustration and fear as Duane managed to get to his feet. He pointed the gun at her. They were now no more than eight feet apart. She could see the gleam in his eyes, feel the hatred and anger coming off him in waves.

"This isn't the way I wanted to end it," Duane said from between clenched teeth.

The wind was whistling through the foot-bridge. That, Billie Rae realized, was why Duane was unaware of Tanner moving stealthily along the bridge behind him. When she'd called, "Stay back," Duane had thought she was warning *him*.

She fumbled in her pocket for the last

cartridge. Duane was watching her almost in amusement. He would never let her load the taser before he shot her and they both knew it.

He took a step forward. She could tell he didn't want to pull the trigger and end it so quickly. He wanted to hurt her. Worse, if he shot her, how would he explain it? But she knew when push came to shove, he would shoot her before he'd let her taser him again— and that could be as much justice as she could get.

"I gave you everything," he said, pain in his voice. "You were my wife. I treated you like a princess."

"A princess you slapped around when you had a bad day," she snapped unable to hold her tongue as she was forced to hang on to the rope with one hand and frantically try to load the taser with the other.

He stopped now only a few feet from her. "I used to watch my old man slap my mother around. I hated him for doing it. But I didn't realize that women push you to hurt them."

"We ask for it, right?"

"Make fun, but Billie Rae, if you had tried harder not to set me off—"

"Stop lying to yourself, Duane. You liked beating up a defenseless woman," she pushed. "It made you feel like you were somebody."

His face twisted in anger. He raised the gun so she was looking down the dark hole of the barrel. "I'm sorry it has to end like this. I really am."

Just pull the trigger. Let's get this over with because I can't live like this anymore. "Yeah, too bad you didn't get to slap me around some more, huh, Duane?"

The face she'd once found handsome twisted into the monster he was. "Goodbye, Billie Rae." He grabbed for her with his free hand, his intent in his eyes. She was going off the bridge. Alone.

TANNER HEARD WHAT DUANE SAID as he came up behind him. As he swung the tire iron, the cop must have felt the movement behind him or sensed his presence. He half turned, catching the blow on his shoulder.

The sound of the report from the handgun echoed in the narrow canyon, but all Tanner heard was Billie Rae cry out. Duane fell back against the rope rail and almost toppled over, but caught himself.

He'd managed to still hang on to the gun as he half turned, knocking the tire iron out of Tanner's hand. It fell to the bridge and Tanner lost sight of it.

As Duane turned the gun on him, Tanner grabbed for it and they wrestled on the bridge, making it rock crazily. Tanner's gaze shot past Duane to the spot where he'd last seen Billie Rae.

She was gone.

THE CARTRIDGE LOCKED IN the taser just an instant before Duane grabbed for her. He got a handful of her jacket in his big fist before she could raise the weapon and fire.

She saw his expression and knew that he had sensed Tanner coming up behind him because he only had time to shove her through the ropes of the bridge railing before he was turning to fire again.

Billie Rae saw it all in those few heart-dropping moments. As she fell off the edge of the bridge through one of the spaces between the ropes, she stuffed the taser back into the jacket pocket and closed her eyes.

She could feel the fear contort her face as she fell—not at all sure she would stop before she hit the river fifty feet below. The drop was no more than a few yards, but when the climbing rope attached to her harness caught and she stopped falling, the impact was more jarring that she'd thought it would be. It knocked the air out of her.

She dangled from the bridge cable high above the gorge and fought to breathe. She didn't dare look down. Above her through the bridge slats, she could see Duane and Tanner wrestling for the gun. Still gasping for breath, she reached up and began to ratchet herself back up toward the bridge like the clerk at the climbing store had showed her.

He had made it look so easy on the store climbing wall. It took all her effort to rise the few feet to the level of the bridge, the effort more difficult because of the growing wind. But all she could think about was Tanner. She had desperately needed him the night of the rodeo. Now he desperately needed her.

Just before Duane had thrown her off the

bridge, she'd heard the report of his gun. But she hadn't realized he'd shot her until she looked down and saw that the jacket was soaked with blood.

She realized she was losing a lot of blood because suddenly she felt light-headed. She clung to the climbing rope as the bridge above her blurred. Just a little farther. Tanner and Duane were still fighting for the gun. She felt as if she could pass out at any moment.

Pushing herself, she ratcheted herself up the last few inches. As she reached the edge of the footbridge, she pulled out the loaded taser and prayed for a clear shot.

As they fought for the gun, Tanner knew he was fighting for his life. It was almost impossible to keep from losing his balance and falling from the bridge. Duane was strong and wild with an insane need to finish what he'd started. Tanner fought with a craziness of his own, believing that Duane had already killed Billie Rae.

He found himself thrown against the rope railing as they grappled for the gun, the bridge threatening to spill them both into the river far below. Duane kneed him in the groin and Tanner stumbled back, falling to the floor of the footbridge. He would have fallen through the opening had he not managed to grab hold of one of the vertical ropes and get one leg wrapped around the wooden slats on the opposite side.

He was breathing hard from the exertion and the near fall when he looked up to find Duane standing over him. Duane had the gun in one hand and was hanging onto the bridge rope rail with the other. He was breathing hard, sweating, but smiling as he pointed the weapon at Tanner's chest.

Tanner saw the tire iron caught between two of the wooden slats of the footbridge floor. Duane saw it too and slammed down his foot on it before Tanner could grab it.

"You should never have come between me and my wife," Duane said. "Let alone assault a police officer with a weapon," he added as he kicked the tire iron off the bridge. He seemed to watch its descent out of the corner of his eye and Tanner knew exactly what the cop had in mind for him once he shot him.

Like the tire iron, he would be making that fifty-foot fall to the rocks and river below them.

That's when behind Duane, Tanner caught a glimpse of Billie Rae dangling from the bridge. Tanner had never been so happy to see Billie Rae. She was bleeding but he couldn't tell how badly she'd been hit.

With a start, he understood the climbing rope and why she'd attached the end of it to the steel cable. She had been expecting that very thing to happen.

The woman was crazy.

Of course she was. Her husband had driven her to this point where she felt she had nothing to lose.

Tanner thought of her in his arms, her face in the light from the fireworks, the look she'd given him yesterday just before she'd left. She'd known that she couldn't run far enough from the man she'd married. She'd known that one day she would have to end it because if she didn't Duane would kill her.

He couldn't imagine having that kind of monkey on his back.

Duane thrust the gun out in front of him

as he took a more careful aim for Tanner's heart. "It was a shame that I had to kill you. But after what you did to Billie Rae. The jealous lover pushing Billie Rae off the bridge when she told you she would never leave her husband."

"Do you really think that will fly?" Tanner said.

"You forget, I'm a cop."

BILLIE RAE CLUNG TO the edge of the swaying bridge, the wind in her face, her vision blurring from the loss of blood. She felt lightheaded and feared she might pass out at any moment.

The battle between the two men had driven them both away from her. Duane was a good fifteen feet away from her now—on the edge of the taser range.

But there was nothing she could do about that. She was feeling faint and her arms were trembling from the climb up the rope. She felt as if she was going into shock.

Billie Rae thought about calling down the bridge to Duane to get his attention, but she didn't dare chance it.

She raised the taser and tried to steady it. The last cartridge was loaded. If she missed him—

Duane was clinging to the rope with one hand, the gun in the other aimed at Tanner's chest. She could hear the hum of his voice but she couldn't make out his words. There was no doubt in her mind he intended to kill Tanner, who was lying on his back unable to do more than cling to the moving floor of the footbridge.

Everything began to fade from her vision. She felt herself getting weaker, the taser slumping a little in her hands as the bridge rocked and her eyes dimmed.

She said a silent prayer and pulled the trigger.

TANNER HAD SEEN BILLIE RAE holding the taser. He could see that she was struggling to aim it.

"Any last words?" Duane asked.

"Burn in hell," Tanner said. The darts caught Duane in the low back. He fell against the rope railing and for a moment Tanner thought his weight would snap it—or flip the bridge and both of them off it.

The floor twisted and Tanner was looking down at the water below him. The river was dark now that the sun was lower in the sky, but the rocks just beneath the surface still shone like sun-bleached bones as the water rushed over them.

Duane seemed to teeter on the rope, his body bent over it. Tanner grabbed the weapon Duane dropped and now held it on the man suspended on the rope.

He would later remember it all happening in an instant. Duane suspended there. And then in a blink, gone.

But right now it seemed to happen in slow motion. Duane's heavy body looped over the rope, making the bridge twist to the side, before gravity finally claimed the weight of his limp body. Tanner impulsively grabbed for him as Duane fell over the side of the bridge. But there was no saving him from the river—or from himself.

Then there was only the sound of the wind but he knew that like him, Billie Rae was listening for the moment when Duane landed in the river below them. He saw her hanging like a limp doll from the climbing rope, her gaze blurred with tears.

Tanner listened, but there was nothing to hear over the wind.

He didn't look down either as he made his way toward Billie Rae. She seemed to watch him through her tears. And then he was pulling her up and into his arms and holding her and telling her not to worry.

"Everything is going to be all right."

In the distance he could hear the sound of sirens headed this way as Billie Rae slumped in his arms.

Chapter Fourteen

"I can't believe Emma would do this," Tanner said as he looked around the kitchen table at his brothers. The six of them had gathered at the main house after Marshall had discovered Emma missing.

Dawson shoved the note across the table. "Believe it. It's right there in black and white."

"She took all her things," Marshall said. "Her closet is cleaned out. Everything is gone."

Tanner shook his head. "This is going to break Dad's heart."

"How is Billie Rae?" Dawson asked, changing the subject.

"The bullet wound missed any vital organs," Tanner said. "The doctor is releasing her today."

"The police cleared the two of you?" Dawson asked.

He remembered the hours of questioning, the days of worrying about Billie Rae, the awful time spent next to her hospital bed fearing she might not survive. "McCall said it shouldn't be too long before the investigation is concluded and Billie Rae and I are exonerated."

"What is Billie Rae going to do now?" Zane asked.

"Go back to North Dakota for the time being." Tanner had wanted to go with her but she'd insisted she needed to do this alone.

"I can't believe the judge denied bail and Dad has to stay in jail until his trial," Logan said.

"The judge thought he was a flight risk." Colton had been quiet until then. The fact that he was engaged to a sheriff's deputy didn't make him all that popular right now.

"As if Dad would ever leave the ranch," Logan said and looked to the others as if needing to be reassured.

"Dad didn't kill anyone," Dawson snapped, getting to his feet. "Enough sitting around here moping. Emma is gone. We have to finish the fence. I'll go into town for the load of barbed wire. The rest of you get ready to string fence for the next few days. This ranch isn't going to run itself and we have no idea of how long before Dad is cleared and back home."

"Any word on those rustlers that were hitting ranches down by the Wyoming border?" Zane asked.

Dawson shook his head. "I'll ask around while I'm in town. But I can tell you right now, they won't be getting any of our cattle."

"I'm going by the hospital to see Billie Rae and then I'll catch up with you out in the north forty," Tanner said and watched his brothers file out of the house.

He stood for a moment, listening to the silence. It hadn't been this quiet since Emma had come into their lives. He missed her, missed the rich aroma of whatever she had baking in the big kitchen. She'd made the house warmer, made their lives warmer as well.

Tanner still couldn't believe she would turn tail and run at the first sign of trouble. It just didn't seem like her, he thought as he picked up the note off the kitchen table and reread it.

I'm sorry but I can't do this,
Emma

No matter what the others said, Tanner knew his father was going to be heartbroken. Emma had been the love of his life.

CINDY ROSS FIDGETED in the seat across from the sheriff. "I got your message?" She made it sound like a question. She smelled of soap and her hair was still wet from her early morning shower.

McCall could see the fear in the girl's eyes and wished she had better news. "We haven't found your aunt. As you know we found her rental car." She didn't mention the blood they found on the seat. McCall was still waiting for forensics to tell her whether or not it was Agatha Wells's blood. The lab was testing the blood stain against hair follicles found in a hairbrush in the suitcase.

Cindy's eyes widened in alarm. "You aren't going to stop looking for her, are you?"

The team dragging the river had discontinued their search for Aggie Wells. "Law enforcement will continue to keep an eye out for your aunt."

"That's it? That's all you're going to do?" the girl asked, sounding close to tears.

"Until we get another lead—"

"What about that body you found out there?" Cindy asked.

McCall wasn't surprised the girl had heard about the remains found near her aunt's abandoned car. "That is tied in with another case."

"I know you arrested Hoyt Chisholm for the murder of the woman's remains you found. It was one of his wives that he murdered. He's going to prison, isn't he?"

"The remains were identified as one of his wives, but until his case goes to trial—"

"You know he killed my aunt."

She didn't know that. But like everyone else in town, she suspected he might have. "Have you been in contact with your father?" McCall asked the girl, seeing how upset she was.

"He hasn't heard from her." From the way she ducked her head, McCall guessed the father wasn't happy about his daughter's coming to Whitehorse in search of her aunt, let alone her staying so long.

"You might consider going home," the sheriff said. She knew Cindy had been staying at a local motel, waiting for news of her aunt. "When we have any news of your aunt…" If they ever did, but she didn't say that.

Cindy had slumped in her chair, all the fight gone out of her.

"Do you have money to get home?" McCall asked.

"I have enough to catch the bus back," she said. "I just feel like I should stay here, though, in case—"

"Your aunt will expect you to be in Arizona, right? That will be the obvious place she would try to contact you."

The girl lifted her head, hope shining in her eyes. "You still think she might be alive?"

"We have no evidence otherwise at this point." McCall didn't want the girl to be so far away from her father when there was news about her aunt. After this much time and what they'd discovered on the seat of Aggie Wells's abandoned rental car, McCall wasn't expecting the news to be good.

BILLIE RAE WAS DRESSED and standing at the window when she heard Tanner come into the hospital room. She knew the sound of his boots on the hospital's tiled floor after all his visits over the days she'd been healing.

She had a lot more healing to do—and not just from the gunshot wound.

As she stared out at the beautiful Montana summer day, she heard him come up behind her. She ached to feel his arms around her, the touch of his lips against her skin, the whisper of his voice next to her ear.

She turned before he reached her, knowing how easily he could destroy her resolve. "I was just thinking about you," she said honestly.

"That's a good start," he said, his Stetson in his sun-tanned callused hands. He'd been working at the ranch when he wasn't coming to the hospital to see her. He looked stronger, his shoulders seeming broader. There had always been strength and integrity in this man. She'd seen it that first night at the rodeo.

But now there was something different about him. A calm assuredness—and she knew it had something to do with how he felt about her.

He could survive without her, though. She wasn't so sure she could without him.

"I'll come back," she said, her voice breaking as she looked into his handsome face and fought the urge to reach out and feel the smooth line of his freshly shaven jaw beneath her fingers.

"I'm planning on that," he said.

She met his warm brown gaze, saw how hard it was for him to let her go. But he'd helped free her of a man who had tried to hold on to her at all costs. Tanner would let her go—even if it broke his heart—and that was what she loved so much about him.

All the hours he'd spent visiting her while she was in the hospital, he'd talked about everything but the two of them and the future. He'd known she wasn't ready for that.

"I should get going. I'm taking the train back to Williston."

"Do you need a ride to the station?" He sounded so hopeful, she almost weakened. But she couldn't bear another goodbye, especially one in a train station. This was hard enough as it was.

"I have a ride, but thank you."

At a sound behind him, Tanner turned to see his brother Marshall standing in the doorway. When he turned back to Billie Rae, he was smiling. "You couldn't have picked a better person to take you to the train." Then he stepped to her and gently brushed aside a lock of her hair to press a kiss to her forehead before stepping back. "You'd better get going. See you soon. Drive careful, Marshall."

Epilogue

When Tanner saw Billie Rae coming across the field, he thought he must be seeing things.

He'd imagined her coming back to the Chisholm Ranch so many times, this time didn't seem real.

He stood watching her, the sun beating down on him. He'd warned himself that it might be months before she'd come back. There was also the possibility that she wouldn't. She might want to forget everything about what had happened on the bridge that day—and him with it.

Sheriff McCall Crawford had stopped by to tell him that the investigation of Duane Rasmussen's death had been completed. Both he and Billie Rae had been cleared of any wrongdoing. Duane's body had been released, his remains cremated and sent to Billie Rae in Williston.

So many times Tanner had wanted to turn his pickup down Highway 2 toward North Dakota. He'd wake up in the middle of the night knowing that Billie Rae had cried herself to sleep. He couldn't bear thinking of her alone back in Williston and being forced to come to terms with Duane's death and the ashes of her marriage.

But he'd done what she'd asked and he'd waited, counting the days, then the weeks, watching and waiting for her, planning what he would say when he saw her again. He'd hoped she would call, but she hadn't.

In all that time, there had been no word from Emma, either. Tanner still thought it odd. They all missed her and had moved back into the main house to hold down the fort until the day their father was set free.

It had been a waiting game. The only thing that had saved him was work. They had put in miles of new fence posts and were still stringing barbed wire along with all the other chores of running such a large ranch.

Now as Billie Rae walked the rest of the

way across the pasture to where he was leading an appaloosa mare back toward the corral,
words failed him.

Billie Rae looked so beautiful. Her face
seemed to glow in the morning sunlight. Her
brown eyes shone with tears as she stopped a
few feet from him, looking almost shy. Then
she smiled and he realized he didn't need any
words.

Tanner let out a whoop, dropped the horse's
reins and ran to her. He picked her up by her
waist and swung her around in a circle before
slowly lowering her down to the ground.

He looked into the depths of her gold-
flecked brown eyes and saw love shining out.
"Welcome home, Billie Rae."

She smiled through her tears and it could
have been the Fourth of July all over again.
Tanner swore he felt fireworks exploding
around them as he pulled her into his arms
and kissed her.

BILLIE RAE KNEW the moment she saw his
face that this was where she belonged—in
Tanner Chisholm's arms. And then he kissed
her and she couldn't believe how far she'd

come from that night in July when she'd been running for her life and Tanner had caught her.

Fate? Maybe. Love at first sight? Definitely. She remembered looking up into the cowboy's face and feeling safe for the first time in months.

In the weeks since what had happened on the bridge, she'd struggled with her heart. If it had had its way, she would never have left Whitehorse or Tanner. But her head said she needed time. She had to go back to Williston and take care of the mess she'd made of her life by marrying Duane.

Billie Rae had also wanted time to be sure that what she felt was real. Now as she drew back from the kiss to cradle his face in her hands and look into his eyes, she couldn't imagine anything more real.

"There is something I need to tell you," she said.

He laughed and shook his head. "I love you too, Billie Rae Johnson."

She smiled. "That too." She brushed a lock of his hair back from his forehead and turned serious. Just last week she'd gotten the tests back. "How do you feel about being a father?"

His brown eyes lit up and he let out another whoop as he picked her up again and spun her in a circle.

"Put that woman down!" Marshall called as he came out the back door of the main house.

"Billie Rae and I are havin' a baby!" Tanner called back.

"Isn't that putting the cart before the horse?" Marshall asked, grinning as Tanner led Billie Rae over to him.

"She might be a little gun-shy of marriage," Tanner said, eyeing her. "But I was about to ask her." He got down on one knee. He'd been carrying the ring around in his pocket for weeks like a good luck charm. "Marry me and make me the happiest man in Montana."

Billie Rae let her heart answer.

* * * * *

LARGER-PRINT BOOKS!
GET 2 FREE LARGER-PRINT NOVELS PLUS
2 FREE GIFTS!

Harlequin

INTRIGUE

BREATHTAKING ROMANTIC SUSPENSE

HILP11

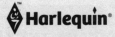